LEAVING THE
PIECES BEHIND

LEAVING THE PIECES BEHIND

R.M. Demeester

Leaving The Pieces Behind
© 2019 R.M. Demeester
Published in Canada
ISBN: 9781999404727

Prologue

Fifteen years prior…

At eight in the morning, my alarm went off. I would have woken up earlier, but Mom didn't like us up before eight. She always said she needed her quiet time, and I didn't want to upset her. I climbed down the steps and pulled on the frilly red dress the lady at church made me for my birthday. I was turning eight today. I had counted the days until I would no longer be seven. I figured, why be seven when you could be eight? Being a year older would make me even more mature. I was so excited, which is why I didn't understand why Mom didn't like her birthday. A few months ago, Harmony and I sang her a song for her birthday, but I don't think she enjoyed it as much as we did.

I hovered over my little sister, Harmony, and shook her. "Wake up."

She turned and stared at me with one eye open, then groaned. "Whaaat?"

"Get up!" I climbed on the first step to the top bunk, grabbed my pillow, and threw it at her.

She half screeched, half whined. "Don't!"

I giggled and ran out of the room and down the hall to the living room. My eyes widened. Mom had blown up balloons and attached them to the walls with tape. I turned on the light in the kitchen. Pink streamers hung from the ceiling around the fan. On the wall behind the table, Mom had written *Happy Birthday* in large letters on some leftover scraps of paper. Nearby, an empty tin can, which I had decorated with glitter and stickers, held the markers my mother bought me for Christmas last year.

Mom entered the kitchen, and I hugged her tightly.

"Happy Birthday, Serenity," she said.

Mom looked tired. She barely smiled. I didn't say anything else because I could tell she hadn't slept last night. I wished she were happy, especially today of all days.

Mom staggered to the counter and opened the fridge to reveal a delicious-looking chocolate cake. My eyes lit up. I didn't think Mom would have had enough money to buy one.

She smiled. "You can thank the kind ladies down the street for making it for you."

Soon, Dayton and Harmony staggered into the kitchen.

"I'm hungry," Dayton howled. "I want my birthday!" I wanted to throw something at him. I never complained about things on his birthday.

Mom turned and stared at Dayton. "Quit your whining and take a seat."

She brought the cake to the table. "Sorry I don't have any birthday candles."

She reached into the cupboard and grabbed three plates, then put them in front of each of us. "I don't feel like making breakfast, so you can have cake instead."

She plopped a large piece of cake in front of Harmony. It didn't matter that it was my birthday; if Harmony didn't get hers first, she'd cry like a big baby. She had to make everything about her. It wasn't fair. But it was just what she did. Mom sat in the empty chair and glared at the back wall. What was she thinking about?

"Mommy," Harmony whined. When Mom didn't respond quickly enough for her, she screeched louder. "Mommy!"

"What?" Mom shouted. Harmony's bottom lip jutted out and her face contorted into a pout. Mom took a deep breath. "What, Harmony?"

"Can I have a drink?" she said in an almost whisper.

"Yeah, me too," Dayton added.

Mom stood and walked toward the fridge, then stopped. She stared at a large box on the counter.

"What's that?" I asked, hoping it was something for me.

Mom picked up the box and headed back to the table. "A present for your birthday." She stood for a few more moments. "Why don't you open it while I go lay down? Keep Harmony and Dayton out of trouble."

Without another word, she left the kitchen and headed toward her bedroom. I guess she forgot to get Dayton and Harmony their drinks.

I shrugged and opened the box. Buried beneath pink tissue paper was a toy purse with accessories.

Harmony reached over to take it from my hands, but I pulled it away. "It's mine."

She whined loudly.

"Shh!"

"I want it!"

I went to hand it to her, just so she wouldn't upset Mom, but I was too late.

Mom entered the room again. "Harmony, be quiet!" she ordered, frowning, her hands on her hips.

"Sorry, Mommy."

Mom ignored her, turned, and looked at me. "Didn't I tell you to keep them occupied?"

I bowed my head, apologizing. She huffed and turned back toward her room. I hated being the oldest. I pouted. I didn't want to share my stuff or spend all my time babysitting.

***

Two weeks had passed since my birthday. Today I had school, and once again I woke myself up in the morning. This week, Mom had slept a lot. She wasn't feeling good. Harmony and Dayton were sick as well, so she had an especially hard time getting up in the morning. I picked up the crumpled jean dress off the floor and put it on. I knew Mom would get around to washing our clothes eventually. Harmony cried from the bottom bunk. "I don't feel good."

Mom hovered over her. "Now, now."

Then, across the hall, Dayton screeched at the top of his lungs. Mom left the room to help him.

I looked at Harmony, and her bottom lip pouted. "I don't want to go to school."

The alarm clock read five after eight. I had to hurry to catch the bus. I rushed past Mom's bedroom.

"Make sure to brush your hair!" Mom called from across the hall

"I did," I lied.

"Okay, sweetie. I'll pick you up after school."

I walked into the kitchen and opened the cupboard to grab a snack, but there were none. I looked on the second shelf, behind an empty container. The jar of grocery money that Mom kept back there was still full. She hadn't gone shopping yet. If only Harmony and Dayton were feeling better, we would have food in the house.

I ran for the bus. Today there was a spelling test, something I was good at.

When I walked into the classroom, some of the girls stopped and stared at me as I walked to my desk. I avoided their glances, but I knew what they were thinking. *Loser.* They stared at me and made comments about my dress. I was poor, and everyone knew it.

"Spelling test first thing. Everyone, take out a piece of paper and write your name at the top," my teacher, Mrs. Anderson, said. She looked around the room, her eyes meeting mine. She was one of the few people in my life who didn't treat me like I was invisible. She had come to my aid so many times when bullies picked on me, and she always asked me how my day was. She was almost like a second mommy.

She listed off words one by one. I spelled them with ease.

Then, one by one, we headed up to her desk to hand in our tests. When it was my turn, I smirked. I knew I was going to get an *A*. I always got an *A*. Mommy would be so proud of me. Maybe when she got her next paycheck, she'd buy me that fancy pencil and eraser set I wanted.

Later that day, at recess, Chelsea—whose house my mom used to clean before Chelsea's mother fired her—was standing right outside the entrance of the building with all the other rich kids. Chelsea whispered to her friend, loud enough so I could hear. "She is such a loser."

I tried to walk away, but Chelsea and her friend started following me.

"Where are *you* going?"

"Inside."

"She's going to help the teacher."

"Teacher's pet! Teacher's pet!" Chelsea chanted over and

over again as I ran into the school.

It was like any other day, but at that moment, my heart filled with dread.

The bell rang at 3:10 PM on the dot. I ran out the door and down the hall, but Mom wasn't there. I sat on the steps and waited. I figured she was probably running late, especially since Harmony and Dayton were sick. I watched as other parents arrived and picked up their kids. The teachers helped the students into their parent's cars, but no one paid any attention to me.

Then, my neighbor, Charlotte, showed up. She was a funny old lady who lived next door. She had a crooked smile and a kooky laugh. All the neighborhood kids made funny jokes about her.

"Serenity."

I walked up to her. "Where's my mom?"

"She couldn't make it. I'll explain later."

"No, tell me now!" I demanded. Where was my mother? Where was she?

She frowned. Her face lost all its color. She ushered me into her car, ignoring my pleas.

"Where's my mom?" I asked her when she got in on her side.

She mumbled something and told me in a stern voice that I'd find out later.

The ride was silent. Dead silent. I was shaking, my heart racing. *Why wasn't she telling me anything?* I wanted to know where Mom was. *Please let her be okay. Please let her be okay. I'm sure she'll be fine.* I finally decided Mom was probably just too busy to come. She'd forgotten before.

When we pulled up in front of my house, I saw a police car out front.

"Why are they here?" I asked.

Then, I noticed Dayton and Harmony standing outside beside Charlotte's husband. Dayton was pulling as hard as he could, his face beet-red, but he couldn't break free from her husband's grasp.

I opened the car door and ran up to him. "Let go of him! Let go of him!" I screamed, trying to pry my brother away.

Dayton stared at me with his eyes wide open. "Help me," he pleaded.

Harmony looked at her feet, not saying anything.

"Where's my mom?" I asked again.

When no one answered me, I ran toward the house but was stopped by a police officer as he stepped out the front door.

Inside the house, I heard my mom crying. "Don't take my babies! Don't take my babies!"

"Mom!"

She choked on her words. "Serenity, I love you baby... I-I..." She couldn't find the word to complete her thought.

At that moment, I froze, waiting. I wanted Mommy to respond. A policeman peeled me away from the door. I was screaming in my head, *Mommy!* But I couldn't speak. Fear froze me to the core.

When they took me to a waiting car, I found my voice. "Where are you taking me?"

The officer smiled. "Don't worry. Everything will be okay."

He could say whatever he wanted. I knew he was lying.

Harmony and Dayton were placed in another vehicle, and suddenly I was all alone.

The ride to wherever I was going was long. I stared out

the window at the passing houses as I left my neighborhood. I couldn't say goodbye to my mom or Harmony or Dayton. Not even the few friends I did have. We reached a highway, and I remembered travelling down this road when we moved here.

"Where are we going?" I asked again. "Where's my mommy?"

The lady who was driving looked at me in the mirror. "To your new home," she responded without the slightest hint of a smile. She didn't make me feel good. *New home? What was wrong with my house?*

I didn't ask any more questions until we pulled up to a house.

A tall woman with curly hair answered the door.

The lady who drove stared at me. "This is Mary. Be a good girl for Mary. I'll check on you in a few days, all right?"

They ushered me into the house, and the lady handed me a small suitcase. After a few minutes, I was taken to a small bedroom.

That night, I cried myself to sleep.

I just wanted to go home.

Chapter 1

Since I lost my job at George's Bakery, my life had gone to shit. For the last few months of my employment, the business was slow. The owner plucked all the bakers one by one, like chickens with their heads cut off. I did more than expected, but it wasn't enough. Like the others, I received my walking papers.

My roommate, Sophia, knocked on the door, disturbing my floundering. "Serenity, rent is due this Friday, so don't forget!"

"I know." I scowled. As if I needed the reminder. Money, or the lack of it, was always on my mind.

I had no money to my name after bailing my brother out of jail. Dayton really pissed me off. He had royally screwed me over.

I paced around my room, wondering how I could have been so stupid. Growing up, he constantly lied to get what he wanted. Why would this time be any different? I'd never forget the day he called me from jail. That should have been a red flag, considering where we came from and the life we both lived, but this time he sounded as if he would cry.

"Please, Serenity. I'll lose my job if you don't help me," he whined. Like an idiot, I believed him and bailed him out.

Coming back to the present, I clenched my fists, the whites in my knuckles showing. My own brother used me. I should be accustomed to it by now.

I leaned against the wall by the window, at just the right angle that enabled me to steal my neighbor's Wi-Fi signal. I couldn't afford my portion of the internet bill, and so my roomies had changed the password on me. After I got my signal, I scrolled through the job listings which didn't require years of experience. I stopped at one: *Local Business, Cashier Wanted*. I could do that.

Thirty hours a week, eight-fifty an hour. I did the math in my head. It was more than I would make with unemployment.

No time like the present. I figured I'd head down there and apply in person. I grabbed a resume from my top dresser drawer before strolling out of the room, down the hallway and to the front door. I was careful not to make eye contact with any of my housemates. They already didn't like me, and the feeling was mutual. Feeling like an intruder in your own home was a familiar sense.

On the way to the bus stop, I passed several boarded-up businesses and houses not fit for living. It only reminded me of how much I hoped I could afford to move somewhere else one day.

With moments to spare, the bus pulled up to the curb, and I stepped aboard. I took a seat behind a pair of elderly ladies.

"Susan is getting married this weekend," one woman said to the other, and they soon began to gossip.

The pit in my throat pulsed. I had accepted that getting married wasn't my reality, and if it were, it wouldn't be the perfect-picture day everybody talked about. My family wasn't the type to marry. Three generations of women, and not a husband in sight.

My gaze shifted out the window to escape any more

painful uncertainties.

The bus slowly stopped, and a group of people piled on. I shuffled over to allow a man wearing an oversized army jacket to sit. The musty scent of cheap bourbon and cigars radiated off him. I moved as close to the bus wall as I could, holding my breath while calculating the number of blocks to the terminal.

As the bus came to a stop, I hurried off. Quickly, I accessed the downtown internet to look up the address again. It was four blocks away; quicker to walk than wait for another bus.

Still looking at my phone, I crossed the street as a semi took an abrupt turn, missing me by a sliver.

I sucked in a deep breath. That was too close. I briskly walked, holding my chest as my racing heart subsided.

I reached the address. The closed sign was lit up in bright red letters. On closer inspection, a quickly written note was stuck underneath the sign: *Please insert resume here.* I deposited my resume into the slot.

Exhaling with relief, I turned and headed toward home, walking more calmly this time. The fresh air was wonderful, and I needed to get used to walking. My bus pass would soon expire, and I wouldn't have the money to renew it.

Why did my life have to suck so bad?

The realization set in. My eyes filled with tears at the thought of tomorrow. I staggered down a back alley, stumbling as if drunk. My shoulders sagged beneath the weight of my own debt. What was coming next? What was I going to do? How could I make money? No one was hiring me. The economy sucked. There were no rich fathers to pay my bills, no sugar daddy to ensure I didn't end up homeless. I had nothing and no one but myself to rely upon.

At the end of the alley, I took a deep breath and wiped away my tears. I had to stop being a baby. Crying never helped. Crying had never gotten me anywhere. All I could do was pull up my big girl pants and deal with it. Nobody was coming to my rescue, and that was that. The system took me from my mother and abandoned me in the care of strangers. Once I turned eighteen, even that small comfort was taken from me.

They'd said I was on my own.

A slight early evening breeze wafted through the air, calming me. I hoped when I reported home, I'd be alone with no distractions. Maybe I'd have a bath or sneak something to eat.

I didn't see him when we smashed into each other. He lost his balance and his briefcase fell, papers spilling out.

My heart raced. Embarrassment burned my cheeks. Unable to stop myself, I blurted, "I'm so sorry." I bent down to help the man gather his papers.

He took the stack from my trembling hands. "It's okay, ma'am."

We exchanged glances. His striking cerulean eyes sent a cold shiver down my back.

He shifted foot to foot. "Hey, don't you work at George's?"

I sighed. "No, I was laid off a few months ago." *Great, another painful reminder.*

He frowned. "I thought it was you. I always assumed you made the best cakes. I have gone there a few times, and I haven't seen you. Now I know why."

My heart quivered, and I found myself on cloud nine. Did I receive a compliment from a handsome-looking man in a form-fitting business suit? The only thing that would make this occasion better was a job landing in my lap.

"Have you applied at West Hill Bakery?"

His words raised my spirits. Did he read my mind? Maybe this day would turn out all right.

"I did, but I received no reply."

"What's your name?" he inquired. He stood towering, and I stood stiff and reticent. When I didn't answer, he quickly added, "I'm friends with the owner. I'll put in a good word."

Holy shit, this can't be real! My mouth opened, but no sounds came out.

"Sorry," he said, and held out his hand.

I returned the gesture, fingers trembling and wrist limp.

"My name is William. Should have known better and introduced myself, being a stranger and all."

"I'm Serenity. Serenity Rupert." My voice was rough, and I drew in a sharp breath, struggling for my poise.

I could have sworn he swallowed hard as he pulled a business card from his pocket and passed it to me.

"My cell number is on there. Let's keep in touch. I'm heading to West Hill this afternoon, and I'll put a good word in for you, Miss Rupert."

"Thanks!"

He glanced at his wristwatch. "I'd better get going; I hope you have a good day!"

I blushed, nodding silently. My mind was going a million miles per hour. There was no way I could deliver a rational response. William smiled, turned, and walked down the alley.

What had just happened? Maybe my luck had turned. Something about meeting William gave me hope.

When I got home, I texted the number he had given me,

thanking him again and apologizing for being such a dumbass.

That night, I hardly got any sleep for wondering if my luck had changed. I pinched myself a couple times just to make sure that this wasn't a dream. When I roused in the morning, I had a text from William.

I talked to the owner at West Hill and arranged an interview this afternoon if you're still interested.

Yes, thank you, I responded.

We sent a few more texts back and forth. My gut coiled in hard knots because I wanted to call and properly thank him, but I couldn't afford to pay my phone bill as it was.

I left the bedroom and rushed passed my other disgruntled roommate, Crystal, and into the bathroom before she could get there. I latched the door. Staring in the mirror, the dark circles under my amber eyes disclosed a lack of sleep. I hope William didn't think I was a junkie or something. I turned on the sink faucet and sloshed water on my face. If I had more time, I'd hop into the shower. But time wasn't on my side. Swearing at myself for my lackluster time management skills only reassured me of every darn thing they used to tell me as a child. Maybe I needed to start proving them wrong.

Crystal knocked on the door. "Are you almost done in there?"

"I'll be out in a second," I mumbled, then turned off the nozzle.

I reached into the cabinet drawer and took out Sophia's eye concealer. The only perk of living with her is that we shared almost the same skin tone. I slathered on a layer of concealer under my eyes and a little on my cheekbones, covering my freckles. A few would be all right, but my face was covered with those small, brown specks.

"I really need to use the bathroom, Serenity."

"Coming." I shoved the concealer back in its place and opened the door.

The blonde wannabe-model scooted past me and closed the door behind her. If I hadn't been so desperate for a place to live, I wouldn't have chosen a bunch of college students to bunk up with. I spun down the hallway to the common area.

Sophia was curled up in a little ball, her nose in a book. She glanced up. "Hi, Serenity! Have the rent by Friday."

I didn't respond as I took a seat on the other side of the couch. As if reminding me yesterday wasn't enough. I hated it when she treated me like a nitwit. In the year I had lived here, I paid my rent on time, every month. Who wanted the risk of being homeless weighing down on them? Going from home to home as a child was enough. No one would choose the same fate as an adult.

"Did you hear me?"

My eyes flashed to hers. "Yes, I heard you." I picked up the remote and flipped through the few channels on the television.

"Nothing is on!" she grumbled, flipping the pages of her book. She sank her nails into the paper to create the loudest screeching noise imaginable.

"I heard you," I repeated to divert her. She shot me a dirty look; a sinister energy slithered into the room. I wasn't in the mood for any pettiness.

I got up and headed to my bedroom, the only four walls in the house where I could be alone. My only place of comfort. I lay on my bed and pulled the bedspread over my head. If William hadn't secured the interview, I would have slept in.

But I had to get up.

This job could solve all my problems.

My phone vibrated. I reached over just as a long-distance number flashed on my screen. Likely, it was someone needing money. Something I didn't have. Yet another reminder of my dwindling bank account.

Putting my phone aside, I studied the room for things to pawn. My eyes roamed over the worn discman I'd found in an online ad for free. Then there was my CD player; a gift from some of my foster parents one year. I'd be lucky to receive five or ten dollars for it. Along with the player, I had a dozen CDs in mint condition. Maybe I could earn a dollar a piece for them.

Even if I scraped up enough funds to pay my rent, what would I do for food or a bus pass?

I'd been helping myself to Crystal's produce and a few crackers from the cupboard. So far, she hadn't caught on, and I didn't want to push my luck. I reached into the drawer beside my bed, searching for something to eat. There was no candy or peanuts in sight. My stomach rumbled in agony. I was so hungry.

I still had an hour left before my interview. Maybe if I showed up early, I would make a good impression. I couldn't let William down after putting himself out there for me. An icy chill rushed up my back; just the mere mention of his name swept me off my feet and made me anxious. In a good way, I thought. My mind still couldn't wrap around how someone could do something nice for a stranger, especially a nobody like me.

I sighed and got out of bed, prepared to trek downtown again.

West Hill Bakery was six blocks away on Main and Fifth

Street. I decided walking was best. I trudged along, reenacting what I would say and do when I met him. I froze a block from the bakery as beads of sweat dotted my forehead. I scurried and texted William. I didn't know what the owner's name was, or who to ask for. I moved to stand in front of an accounting corporation.

Five minutes later, he texted me back. *Hank.*

I thanked him, and the weight lifted off my shoulders.

William had come to my rescue again. If I got this job, I'd owe him big time.

I strolled through the doors with five minutes to spare and looked around. An array of loaves and cakes were on exhibit. An older man strode up to the cash register behind the long counter.

"May I help you, miss?"

"Yes. I have an interview with Hank."

I stood up straight and straightened my shoulders. On the outside, I wanted to project confidence, but on the inside, I concealed a tornado of insecurity. If anyone could fuck this up, it'd be me.

"Oh, yes! William told me all about you. Why don't we go to my office for a little chat?"

I grinned, nodding as I accompanied him through the kitchen. The pastry chefs paused and stared as I strolled past. After we reached the office, Hank closed the door and pointed to a chair in front of his desk. "Please have a seat."

I did as directed. He left the room for a moment and returned with a hot beverage and a donut, which he offered to me.

My eyes widened in shock as I reached for it. "Thanks!" Normally, I would have declined, but I was so hungry.

I held the donut between my thumb and middle finger. I'd wait until after the interview to eat it. As much as I wanted to, I knew I couldn't risk looking desperate.

Hank sat down. "So, you worked at George's Bakery?"

"Yes, for two years."

"Why did you leave?"

"I was laid off. A bunch of us were."

He nodded. "I heard you make a good cake."

I smiled at the compliment, warmth spreading across my cheeks. "I've been told that, yes."

My nerves settled a little, although I couldn't help but wonder what else William had said about me.

"If you are still looking for a job, we just happen to have a full-time baker position."

"Yes!" I said, perhaps a bit too eagerly. "Yes, please."

I could have slapped myself for being so darn rude. This man didn't owe me a damned thing.

"Serenity, correct?"

"Yes, Serenity Rupert." My heart fluttered with hope. I could feel the job was already mine.

"How about you start tomorrow, at 5 AM?"

Was this a test? A trick? My throat was dry, but I pressed on anyway. "Sounds great. Thank you!" I nearly croaked. "Thank you so much! You have no idea!"

He frowned as he stood, and we shook hands. "Glad to have you aboard," he added, and showed me back to the front.

Once I was outside, away from the bakery, I did a little dance in pure excitement. I couldn't even give a damn about what anyone thought. I couldn't believe I had a job. My luck was changing, and soon I would be out of the dark hole these past few months had brought me. I proved them wrong. I proved them all wrong.

***

The following morning, my alarm went off at 4 AM on the nose. I forced myself to sit up. Wiping away the sleep from my eyes, I looked out the window at the pitch-black sky. This would take some getting used to. I stumbled out of bed before heading to the bathroom.

I turned on the shower, letting the steam fill the bathroom, then stepped under the scorching stream. I couldn't thank William enough for getting me this job, I thought, as I reached for the shampoo bottle. My body relaxed, melting beneath the warmth. For the first time in too long, I felt alert. Once my hair was clean, I turned off the tap. As much as I wanted to stay, I couldn't be late for work.

I left the house at four forty. Twenty minutes would be more than enough time to walk to the bakery, especially with the streets being deserted. The benefit of early mornings, I guess. In my early years, I walked everywhere. Mom didn't have a license and couldn't afford a bus pass most months. In the middle of winter, we would walk up to ten blocks in subzero weather to the grocery store.

I approached the street the bakery was on. In the distance, a dark-colored car was parked outside of the building. The pit in my stomach ached as I approached.

The driver's door opened.

Maybe it's just the owner or another employee, I thought. I slowed down my pace, inching up to the walls of the building, as far away from the curb as possible.

As I approached the bakery's front door, William stepped out of the parked car with a steaming Styrofoam cup in hand.

"Good morning," he said.

I smiled. "Hello." I was glad to see him, but why was he here? And how did he know I'd be here so early? Of course, Hank must have told him, I convinced myself.

He handed me the cup. "I was on my way to work and saw you walking. My barista made me an extra hot chocolate, so you can have it."

"Thank you." My heart fluttered. "You're so nice to me."

He rubbed the back of his neck and looked away. "Have a good first day. Nice talking to you, Serenity. I'll text you later."

"Talk to you later."

Where did this ray of sunshine come from? It was as if he fell from the sky and landed in my lap. It almost seemed too good to be true.

After he left, I took a few sips of the hot beverage, feeling uneasiness creep up. While it was nice to see him, his motives seemed unclear. He always seemed to be a mystery, coming in at just the right moment. A white knight I knew I didn't deserve. I checked my phone.

I had only a few minutes before my shift and no time to ponder.

Chapter 2

My first day off had arrived after three days of work. My body screamed in exhaustion as if I had been hit by a truck. I knew I shouldn't complain. I was working now, with a steady income, but my body was out of tune. This new routine would take some getting used to. Despite it all, I felt relief. Finally, things were looking up. I managed to gather the funds needed for rent.

The bus pass and cell phone bill would have to wait until the money started coming in.

I spread out on my bed to play a game of solitaire. At this point, it was all the nightlife I experienced anymore.

I wanted to watch television in the common area, but that meant I'd have to deal with Crystal and Sophia. Later, they'd bring home some hot guy from a campus party. They'd show him off, taunting me. Maybe without knowing. I wished I could have a comfortable life like those two, with regular friends and minimal worry about money. Being born into poverty, then taken from my family and tossed from foster home to foster home didn't provide stability. It certainly didn't provide guidance. It didn't allow me to go to school tuition-free, either.

I rechecked my phone. William had texted me again. A fluttering feeling invaded me on the inside. How would I describe William and me? Friends? Soon-to-be lovers? Nah.

He was a guardian angel who stepped into my life at the most random of times, got me a job, and kept coming around. So many people had come and gone from my life, I couldn't keep track of who was there forever, and who was only there for a brief moment. But that didn't stop me from hoping things would be different with him.

I checked the text.

Chocolate or Glazed?

I stared at the text. What a random message. *Did he mean donut?*

I swiftly texted him the question. Maybe that was what he was talking about. We seemed to bond over dessert foods. Or maybe he had a hidden sense of humor. Most of our chit-chat was innocent; a lot of small talk and friendly conversation that wasn't quite flirting. It continued to confuse me, as did the intentions of our budding relationship.

Yes, donut. Which one? I prefer Glazed.

I chuckled and sent back, *Glazed as well.*

At the bakery, chocolate cakes were the top sellers. Even at George's, the amount of chocolate frosting we went through was outrageous. With history repeating itself, I'd been going around smelling like frosting, but day in and day out it becomes repulsive. A glazed donut, on the other hand, delicious. It was the definition of heaven.

Up for a late-night snack… If you're not too busy ☺

I chuckled. Busy! That was funny. I was too poor to be busy doing anything. I wondered what his intentions were. Was he asking me out on a date? Maybe he was hinting at something more. My arms trembled, wondering if he would turn out like the others. The few *men* I had dated just wanted me for one thing, and I wasn't about to give it up so fast. I kept telling myself that I would speak up, even if it meant walking home alone in the dark. However, William might view me in a different light. Or, he might stop talking to me when he realized how shy I was. I bit my lip and responded.

Sure!

I hit my forehead. What was I saying? I had no money. Quick damage control.

How about a walk by the park? I don't have a lot of money.

That's fine.

Okay.

Meet you in twenty, how about in front of the bakery?

I changed into a turtleneck and pair of jeans. Some earrings and an infinity scarf completed my look. I felt compelled to impress him, even if we were just friends — or were we acquaintances? I didn't even know what to call him.

I closed and locked my bedroom door before heading through the living room to the front door.

Sophia sat on the couch.

"Where are you going?" She had a notebook and papers scattered around her.

"Out!"

She shook her head and turned her focus to her school work.

I had my phone in one pocket and a pack of gum in the other, just in case my mouth became dry. Crossing the street, I headed down a deserted side street with burnt-out street lights and boarded up buildings. Halfway down the street, a slight breeze whistled through the trees. I trembled.

Passing an alley, two shadowy figures emerged. The reflection in a parked car mirror revealed them following me. I felt my pace quicken to match the speed of my racing heartbeat. Whoever these people were, I had no doubt they meant trouble.

I was just three and a half blocks from the bakery. I crossed another street, and the footsteps followed. My heart sped up, and goosebumps formed. I told myself to keep calm. Maybe they just happened to be going the same direction I was; it could be a coincidence. My insides twisted as I struggled to accept that improbable possibility. Once again, I crossed the street. Out of nowhere, they sprinted toward me. Panicked, I pulled out my cell phone from my pocket.

My hands shook as if they had a mind of their own. Pulling my phone into my hand as calmly as I could, I tried to dial William's number, hoping he was nearby. The meeting spot was close, so maybe I could have him come this way. Another presence might scare them off. The phone started ringing as I tripped over my feet and landed face first into the pavement. My phone slid several feet away.

You've got to be kidding me! I thought.

A female voice echoed in my ear. "Check her pockets."

I tried to roll away, but a foot to my back stopped that idea. I flailed as a hand dug into my pocket. "Help!" I tried screaming, but a hit to the head silenced me.

"All she has is a pack of gum," another voice shouted.

I heard a loud sigh. "Let's take her phone and get out of here."

The weight lifted off my back as they retrieved my phone and ran off into the night.

For a minute or two, I didn't move. Angry, frustrated tears emerged in the corners of my eyes, but I tried to push them away. The few cars that drove by ignored me. No one seemed to notice the helpless woman lying on the sidewalk; or if they did, they certainly didn't care. I managed to pull myself into a sitting position, staring, dazed. My sleeve was torn and my head throbbed with a dull pain. I wiped away traces of blood on the back of my sleeve.

In the distance, someone or something came toward me.

"Oh my god, Serenity! Are you all right?"

I blinked once, twice. William's fuzzy form emerged in my vision. Where was he a few minutes ago? Where was he when I needed him the most?

"When the call cut out, I came running. Are you okay?" The concern in his voice was uplifting, at least.

"They took my phone." Tears pricked my eyes, blurring my vision. Why was I crying? They didn't hurt me. They took my phone, but they didn't hurt me. The tears finally fell. Another thing I couldn't afford to replace.

He kneeled so we were eye level. "Who's they?"

I shook my head. "I don't know. It was dark. There were two of them." I paused to think. "One was female, for sure. The other one... I don't know. I don't know. It was dark," I whispered. My body quivered. This was what happened when I didn't stay home, where nobody could get to me, where I was safe.

He swung one arm around me and helped me to my feet. "My office is just down the block. We should get you cleaned up."

I nodded in agreement. Anywhere was better than sitting in the middle of the street, feeling sorry for myself. We approached a grand building, with large windows and countless floors. I read the sign: *Johnson's Financials*. So, he worked at an accounting or investment firm. That was more than I knew about him just ten minutes ago.

William pulled a key out of his jacket and fumbled with the lock. With a click, the front door opened. By the wall, he punched a code on the security keypad, disarming the alarm.

"I need to lock the door behind us. It's after hours." He locked the door from the inside before taking my trembling hand and guiding me into the deserted hallway. The office doors were closed and the lights were out.

A man in coveralls with a mop firmly planted in a yellow wheeled bucket emerged from a nearby elevator. "What brings you here tonight? Forget paperwork?"

"No, my friend was robbed on our way to meet."

The janitor glanced at me. "You poor thing. Let me grab the first aid kit. Get her something to drink, why don't ya?"

William walked me a few more feet to a door. "This is my office."

He let me in and pulled out a seat for me. Once again, I thought about how thankful I was for him. As I struggled to catch my breath, William handed me a foam cup from the water cooler. "Here."

Grateful, I accepted and took small sips. The janitor soon returned with a first aid kit in hand.

"Thank you," I tried to say, but ended up mumbling instead.

"Here, clean up the poor gal," the man said, "and be sure to lock up on your way out, Will."

William smiled at him. "I will."

The janitor left, the squeaky wheels of his mop bucket echoing in the hall.

William opened an antiseptic packet. "May I?"

I nodded. He dabbed my forehead, and a stinging sensation followed. I winced.

"I'm sorry," he murmured, "I should have given you a heads up that it might sting."

I shrugged my shoulders. It was common sense, yet he was sensitive to my feelings. I appreciated it. A glimpse of light on this overall depressing night. In the many homes where I'd lived, I never had someone care as much about me, and my feelings, as William did right now.

"It's just a small cut, Serenity. It doesn't look like you'll need stitches." He closed the first aid kit and passed me a clean napkin. I wiped my head; the bleeding had stopped.

"Thanks."

William glanced past me, biting his lip. "I'm sorry," he mumbled, "I should have picked you up from your house. But I..."

"This isn't your fault," I blurted out. "Not even a little."

Our eyes connected, and his mouth opened a fraction. He didn't speak, but he wanted to, I could tell. There was something on his mind, sitting on the tip of his tongue.

"Let me call the police," he said.

My insides twisted. "No, don't call them. I'll be fine. I promise." I tried to smile.

"But, they robbed you."

Ever since the *police* took me away from my home, I didn't trust them. They wouldn't be able to help me anyway. Whoever those two were, they were long gone.

"They won't help anyway. I'll just have to figure out how to replace my phone." I bit my lip. Those two thugs really screwed me over. I felt my face flush, and William touched my shoulder. The tension melted away.

"Would you like me to take you home?"

I looked away. I didn't want to leave for home yet, per se. However, I didn't have the confidence to tell *him* that.

"How about a late-night drink, instead? You're over twenty-one, right?"

It was more like a statement than a question to me.

"Yeah," I felt my cheeks redden for some reason. "I'm over twenty-one."

"Would you like for me to drive you home first to change?"

I glanced down at myself and then back up at him and nodded, feeling small and meek. I looked rough.

"Yes, please."

He locked up and took us to his car, the same one he'd driven on my first day at the bakery when he'd brought me that coffee. William unlocked the passenger door for me and opened it.

Standing there, an instant feeling of *what am I doing* entered my mind. It was dark. I had just been robbed, and yet here I was, getting into the car of someone I didn't know. He had helped me out so many times, but that didn't mean I knew him, or even that he knew me. I looked around at the shadows lurking in every corner. The closest thing to any life were the nightclubs in the ritzy area of the downtown core.

"Everything all right?"

I was brought out of my stupor and stared right at William. Even in the darkness, I could see his frown.

"Yeah, sorry." I sat in his car, praying I hadn't just made a fatal mistake.

We sat in the spot for a few moments in awkward silence, not moving. Why wasn't he driving? My anxiety shot through the roof.

"Where am I going?" William spoke up first.

Relieved, I shot off my address. *Don't be a fool, Serenity.*

"Are you sure you're all right?" he asked as he pulled from the curb.

I nodded. "Just a little headache." Which wasn't a total lie; there was a dull pain in my forehead, threatening to explode into a full-fledged headache.

It didn't take long for William to pull up to my place. He stared out the window at the bungalow, the most beautiful home on the block.

"Nice place," he said.

"Thanks," I muttered. "I'll be right back."

He turned to me and smiled. "Take all the time you need."

I walked into the house to find Sophia playing her classical music on full volume, complete with the luxury of her terrible singing. I walked past her, into the kitchen, to grab a glass of water before heading to my bedroom. *Okay, I'd better not keep him waiting too long.* As I reached into my dresser for a change of clothes, Sophia emerged in the entryway.

"Man, do you look like shit." She stood with her hands on her hips. Observing her pink pajama bottoms and pink spaghetti-strap tank top, I guessed she wasn't heading anywhere tonight. But little did she know, I was going to go out for drinks with a guy. A rich guy at that. How would she feel about that?

"Thanks, I guess." I twirled my fingers in my hair. I didn't have any time left to worry about her.

She shrugged as she passed me into the kitchen, moving to the fridge and opening it. "When are you planning on buying your share of the groceries?" She pulled out a can of soda and stood to stare at me, anticipating an answer.

I glared at her. "When I get paid." God, I don't like her. I really wished she would just move away.

"You don't need to be snarky."

I mumbled an apology, turning my back toward her and

whispering, "Then don't ask stupid questions."

I put the empty glass into the sink and headed upstairs to the bedroom to get changed. Maybe I should stay home. I could explain to William that I had a headache. Just as I was formulating what to say in my head, Sophia turned her godforsaken music on again. My decision was made for me.

Hanging out with William, headache and all, was the better of the two options. I changed into a turtleneck and jeans. Right now, I didn't care to impress anyone. I headed toward the front door where, much to my annoyance, Sophia stopped me yet again.

"Where are you going?" she asked.

"Out."

She sighed. "You come home looking like you got beat up, and there is some strange car out front. I'm just worried, all right?"

I took a deep breath to keep from screaming in her face. Since when did she care?

"Fine. I'm going out with my friend," I finally said.

"Okay, text me later."

I gazed at my feet. "Okay." I didn't want to tell her about my ordeal. Sophia and I weren't friends. Never would be friends. I knew she didn't care if I texted her or not.

Not that it mattered; my phone was gone anyway.

Outside, I got into the car. William was on his phone.

"I've got to go, okay, Mom?" He whispered something else and hung up the phone, then turned his attention to me.

"Is everything all right?"

"Yeah, my mom just called. It's nothing." He paused and smiled. "Are you ready to go?"

"I am, but can we maybe go somewhere a little more private. I'm not dressed to go out."

"Sure," he smiled. "We can drive around and talk, or maybe grab a coffee at the campus café. It's open until one, so we still have time to make it."

"Okay," I said. My stomach twisted. I had mixed feelings about the university, and all the rich kids who attended there, but I didn't want to be rude.

"Great!"

He drove back through downtown, toward the university campus.

"Did you attend school here?" I asked.

"No, but I wish I had. My business partner and I visit this café often because it's one of the only ones in town open so late." I couldn't help but sense a hint of dismay in his voice.

"Why?"

"Family issues."

Before I could ask, not that I wanted to, he changed the subject. "You'll like this little cafe. They sell the best donuts." He paused. "But not as good as the ones you make."

I smiled.

"I'm sure they're lovely."

However, my mind kept going back to a few moments ago. Did he have a troubled relationship with his family, as well? My relationship with my mother was strained these days, but still, I tried. Nobody could replace her, and I couldn't change what happened, as much as I wanted to.

My thoughts returned to his statement. Was I overthinking it?

"And here we are," William announced.

We pulled up to a small, unassuming café between two large buildings near the main campus hall. A few months ago, Sophia had mentioned it was an extension of the culinary arts department. I wondered if the chefs were learning anything. I figured I could put them to the test.

William and I entered. To my surprise, the interior was quaint and charming. There were cute little wooden tables with hard transparent plastic over them and wooden benches. A plaque on the wall said the interior had been made in the workshop on campus.

"Looks like we're the only ones in here," William stated.

"Yup." I wasn't sure what else to say.

Above the counter was a clock. It was quarter to one in the morning, so we had to order quick.

"I'll have water," I told the cashier, almost forgetting I had no money. How stupid could I be to forget that small detail? Payday wasn't for a few more days.

"I've got it," William offered. William went ahead and ordered a dozen glazed donuts and an extra-large coffee. Both the cashier and he stared at me.

"Uh…a-a hot chocolate?"

The cashier muttered a total, and William paid.

"Thanks…again," I said as we went to sit down.

William fidgeted in his seat. "You can stop saying thanks all the time. Can't I just do a nice thing for you? As a friend?"

"A friend?" I questioned him back. All this time, I was trying to put a name to what we called us, but this confirmed it.

"Yeah," he said, as he wrinkled his brow. "We are friends, right?"

"Sorry, yeah. Friends," I answered. My face turned hot.

After an eternity, the cashier brought us our drinks and the donuts, neatly packaged in a brown paper box.

William opened it and handed me one.

"Enjoy."

I took it from his hand and took a bite. The surface was gooey, sugary, and melted in your mouth. "These are pretty good."

"See, I told you."

He shoved half a donut into his mouth. Little bits of the sugary glaze fell around his lips. He wiped his face with his sleeve, and I cringed. Up until this point, I had thought he was all proper. But, it was kind of refreshing — if a little weird — to learn he had a few traits I admired.

We sat and made small talk. I was going through the motions, all the meanwhile staring at him, studying him. There was something mysterious about William. Behind the kindness and the charming personality was something I recognized. He was hiding something. Not something sinister, but something he didn't want to share. Who was I to judge?

Chapter 3

The rest of my weekend dragged on. Friday night, despite a strong beginning, was a bust. After leaving the café, William was distant. His mind was preoccupied, in an entirely different dimension. When he pulled up in front of my home to drop me off, his goodbye was weak. Even his smile and "*Have a good night,*" lacked energy.

I sighed as I walked to work on Monday morning. Passing the corner where those two hooligans had jumped me, my heart sped up. I looked both ways, holding my breath, half expecting one of them to jump out. I kept alert. I glanced at every turn, sprinting past every back alley. The sky was still pitch black, and the early shift almost didn't feel worth it anymore. I arrived at the front door and the supervisor, Zina, let me in.

"Good morning," she said. "You're here early."

I glanced at the clock above the front counter. I'd arrived ten minutes before my shift. Of course. I reached into my pocket, removing my hand when I remembered I no longer had a phone. Zina, no longer concerned, turned to the back of the store. I sat on a wooden bench by the front door, taking a moment to enjoy the calm before the store opened. Some days it got busy in here, and the extra seating was appreciated among customers.

All of a sudden, William's car pulled up. He rolled down

his window and smiled at me through the glass door. I lifted a hand and waved. He returned the motion, rolled up his window, and drove off. I sat there dumbfound. What was that?

After a while, I turned and walked into the back to get changed for my shift. I put on an apron and headed to the workstation beside Zina.

"You can start on kneading the dough."

I nodded. "Okay."

"So, you and that young lad going out?" Zina said. "He's friendly with the owner. I never caught his name, though."

"William. And no, we aren't going out. We're just friends, I think." Were we just friends?

Zina laughed, and I turned to look at her. Her toothless grin stared back. "You don't think I notice him showing up whenever you work? He drives by here every morning."

I flushed red. He had started to drive by a lot of mornings, but he usually stopped and waited for me. This morning was different, but I just couldn't put my finger on why.

"You know, I can tell when a girl is interested." Zina handed me a rolling pin. "I have a daughter. All through school, she had her eyes set on this one guy. Now, she tried to convince me they were just friends, but I knew better. I raised her. Trust me, Serenity. I've been there. I know what it looks like."

I smiled, even though her words hurt. I yearned to have that kind of relationship with my mom. Maybe once I got a new phone, I'd call her. It had been a few months since we'd last spoken. Not because I was busy or anything. I was just a lousy daughter. After one of our conversations, she had stopped initiating them. The shame and the memories were hard for her. No matter how much we fought and made up, we couldn't connect. But I wouldn't stop trying.

I looked down at the dough and sprinkled a generous amount of sticky brown sugar, cinnamon, and a handful of raisins. I liked the smell of cinnamon buns. I remembered that when Mom had extra money, she would make them. It was a rare, sweet treat we all enjoyed. If we were extra lucky, she'd make the creamiest, most luxurious cream cheese icing. Cream cheese was expensive, she said. A rare treat.

Tears threatened to emerge from under my eyelids. I gnawed at my upper lip, trying to ease my nerves. Mom was a touchy subject. The memories were tainted, and the aftertaste left me bitter. I couldn't think of her. Not now. Pushing thoughts of my mother away, I placed the cinnamon buns in the oven to bake.

Zina stared at me sympathetically. She didn't say anything, but she must have sensed the sadness coming from me. Life always had a way of bringing me down. What I needed right now was a hug. For some odd reason, I wanted William to hug me. He'd been kind to me, been there for me in my time of need. A tinge of guilt entered my mind. I didn't want to use him as Dayton had used me.

I started on another batch of cinnamon buns. I had five more to do before the six o'clock crew arrived. At George's, we never made to order, except for large catering orders, which were quite rare. It was always baking for the next day's order. But here, at West Hill, almost everything on display was made the day of. The increased price reflected that. But even then, the loaves of bread and dessert pastries were better quality. That, I couldn't deny.

I rushed through my load, placed the last order into the

oven, and removed the first order I had prepared. The gooey, hot, steaming pan of goodness lifted my despair momentarily. I carefully placed them on a serving tray and filled up the first two rows of the display.

Soon, the next shift gathered in. The back of the bakery filled with morning noise; chaos, with chit chat in every corner. I preferred the first hour of every shift; the peace and quiet was sweet. Now, I had to navigate in the anarchy. Walking around people, trying to complete tasks without crashing or standing in people's way. At eight, we'd open for the day, and that was yet another wave of chaos. I didn't want the confusion today. I wanted peace and quiet. But I needed this job.

The next two hours flew by as I focused on my work instead of my misery. I put the last of my morning pastries in the display before I worked on a significant afternoon order. Every afternoon at two, the local soup kitchen came and picked up a large order of bread. Luckily, I didn't work the day shift, and thus didn't have to deal with them. I just had to make sure everything was prepared.

We didn't have our first customer until an hour after opening. Mondays were our slow day, and so we usually didn't struggle for time to complete everything. On my second day, Zina had said I picked up on the routine quickly. The compliment warmed my heart; I wasn't used to praise.

The rest of the shift flew by, and I finished the last of my clean up by one o'clock. Zina and I left for the day. She walked over to the bus stop, and I wandered around the sidewalk outside the front. I half expected to see William show up. He had to have had a good reason for not stopping to chat this morning.

I paced around for a good while before I said *forget it* and started to head home. This Friday was payday. I only worked three days this pay period, so I would get around two hundred dollars. What would I spend it on? Crossing the street toward my house, I decided I'd buy some groceries. That'd pretty much take up the whole check, and my next check would go for rent and a bus pass. My phone bill would probably go to collections. But what good was paying the bill if I didn't have a phone to use? I had to prioritize. Food, rent, and transportation were necessary, at least until I could back on my feet.

I walked inside, and luckily, no one was home. Finals were around the corner, which meant I'd soon be seeing a whole lot more of those two. I wondered if Crystal would be moving out, since this was her last year of university. I knew Sophia had one more year after that. Maybe we would get a new roommate; one a little more tolerable. I walked into the kitchen and pulled out a jug of milk from the fridge. I'd promised Sophia this morning I'd replace what I ate, but I wasn't planning on it until the end of the month at best.

I changed into sweats and laid on the bed, pulling out my laptop. The other night I'd overheard Crystal give the internet password to one of her university friends, which was just the break I needed. Just the luxury of being able to lay on my bed with internet was freeing in a way I couldn't describe. A small reward for dealing with those two. I scrolled through my emails: random chain and junk mail from the multiple newsletters I'd signed up for. I closed my email and opened messenger. I didn't see the point of having it. My sister, Harmony, was never on since she was kicked out of her last place. Mom didn't have a computer, and Dayton was god knows where.

Just the thought of Dayton made my stomach churn. On a hunch, I typed his name into the search engine. I wonder what he'd been up too. I clicked on the first link, dated last week.

> *Police pulled over a red Pontiac Sunfire for a routine traffic stop west of Lars City at approximately 5 PM on Wednesday. The driver, Reece Stevenson, 32, and passenger, Dayton Rupert, 20, were found to be in the possession of a stolen vehicle. They were arrested without incident. Stevenson was charged with grand theft auto, and Rupert was charged with grand theft auto, probation violation, and a failure to appear. Stevenson was released on a $10,000.00 bond, and Rupert was remanded at Lars City Jail.*

I slammed my laptop shut. Fury invaded me on the inside. Would he ever learn? Would he ever stop making bad decision after bad decision? But at least I knew where he ran off to, the little coward. If I had a car, I'd go confront the weasel. Not that it would do any good. He had no money, and he'd likely block my visits anyway. He would be too embarrassed, and on the off chance he were to talk to me, he'd make me feel sorry for him. He always made me feel sorry for him. It was what Dayton did best.

I stretched out on the bed and stared at the ceiling. Despite what he had done, he wasn't in a good place right now. Those were some serious charges and, no matter what, he couldn't stay out of trouble. He and Mom didn't have a relationship as far as I knew. He blamed her for all his problems. The one time I managed to get all three of us kids and Mom together, it was awkward. Dayton was on his phone, ignoring most of what Mom had to say. Harmony sat cumbersomely, chewing her nails, and I had to keep the conversation going. Otherwise, we'd just be sitting there looking like dummies at lunch.

After I got tired of lying on the bed, I got up and headed into the kitchen. Crystal had returned, sitting at the small table next to the counter. I groaned.

Crystal looked up at me. "Hey."

"Hello."

Crystal turned the page in her textbook. "Sophia said you went out with some guy on Friday night."

"Yeah, William," I said. "He's just a friend."

"She said it looked pretty serious. It's okay. I won't judge."

I swallowed hard and sat down beside her. "He is just a friend, for right now, at least."

Crystal twirled her hair around her fingers tightly. "So how did you and this William meet?"

A knot formed in my throat. I didn't really want to retell the tale of how I ran into him while I was feeling sorry for myself. "He was a customer at George's. He happened to help me find this new job." It wasn't a lie; he did help me land a job at the bakery. It just wasn't the whole truth, either.

"Sounds like a nice guy; should bring him by sometime." She turned back to her textbook.

I stood. "Maybe." I hadn't seen a lot of her this weekend, but I thought for sure Sophia would have brought up how shitty I looked when I came home Friday.

I walked to the fridge to grab something to drink. At least Crystal was in a better mood today. For a moment, inviting William over seemed like a good idea. But I wasn't sure what was up with us; our friendship was complicated. We were complicated. I didn't even know if Friday night was a date or not. We hadn't kissed yet, so maybe he just friend-zoned me. I coughed, nearly choking on my water. I needed to stop torturing myself with all these thoughts.

In the living room, I turned on the television to help drown out all the unwanted feelings. I flipped through the few channels we had and stopped on a cooking show. Maybe I could pick up some new recipe to add to the list of things I'd love to try someday.

The chef was making cheesesteak sandwiches. It made my stomach growl. I wanted a big juicy steak, with a thin layer of fat and a homemade barbeque sauce. I hadn't had one since I went on a date with an ex a few years back. I shook my head, trying to forget all about him. Our break up was something I had erased from my mind and didn't wish to remember.

I was lost in my thoughts when the doorbell rang. Crystal walked past me to the front door.

"Hello, can I help you?"

"I'm looking for Serenity."

I jumped up. It was William.

"And here she is. It's nice to meet you." She turned to face me, winked, then walked back toward the kitchen.

I stood a few feet from the door. He managed a meek smile.

"Can we talk?" he asked.

"Sure, would you like to come in?"

He looked away, nervously.

"Or we could go out somewhere. I just don't have any money or really anything to offer you."

"How about a drive?"

I raised an eyebrow. "All right." I sensed something off in the tone of his voice. He had been there for me so many times since we met; maybe he just needed the favor returned.

In his car, he sat there, his shoulder slumped.

"Is everything all right?'

He cleared his throat; his gaze flitted around the vehicle for a moment. "Yeah. I just needed to apologize for Friday night."

"Why?" I said. I did sense something off when he took me home, but I didn't think the night was bad, except for being robbed and all.

"I just can't get what happened to you out of my mind. I feel responsible."

I placed my hand on his shoulder. He jumped, and I pulled away, murmuring, "Sorry."

Dots of sweat formed on his forehead. "Don't be," he replied. "The thing is, Serenity, I really do like spending time with you. I think we get along really well, but I feel like I'm giving you mixed signals."

My mind went into overdrive. Maybe I would get answers to the questions I had been asking myself since we met. Maybe I'd learn his true intentions.

I rubbed the back of my neck. "What do you mean?"

"I just feel like I'm leading you on." He paused and took a deep breath. "I just got out of a long-term relationship, and it ended badly. Not to dump all my baggage on you, but I kind of swore off women until we met. Until I recognized you from George's. This might sound really, really stupid, and you might think I'm crazy, but I felt this connection to you. Like I could trust you." He stopped and looked around. "I'm sorry." Then he pulled something out of his pocket and sat it on my lap. A cell phone.

"I-I can't accept it."

I tried giving it back to him, but he pushed my hand away.

"It's my old phone, and I want you to have it. How else am I supposed to get a hold of you?"

I shrugged my shoulders. "You know where I live and where I work."

He chuckled. "I'd rather not become a stalker. So, will you accept it, from me?"

I looked at the phone. I really did need one, but I couldn't take it, not after everything he had done for me.

"If it makes you feel any better, it'll make me feel better," he offered. "I'd rather you have it then have it sit around collecting dust. And if you don't accept it, I'll just mail it to your house."

I bit my lip. He wasn't going to take no for an answer. "I really do appreciate it." I reached over to hug him but stopped.

He opened his arms wide and then hesitated for a moment before we hugged awkwardly. When he released my grasp, he looked at his watch. "I hate to cut our meeting short, but I have paperwork to finish."

"Sounds good, and thanks so much. I'll text you when I get it hooked up."

"Have a good day, Serenity."

I got out of the car and waited until he pulled away. I held the phone to my chest, mentally reconsidering my bill plan. I guess the bus pass would have to wait. Now I had a working phone again, thanks to William. After I paid my bill, I would need to figure out a way to make it up to William. To show him my appreciation.

Inside the house, I headed to my bedroom when Crystal came out of the bathroom and stopped me. "He's good looking."

"Yup." I looked away.

Crystal placed her hands on her hips. "If you don't snatch that babe up, someone else will, Serenity. Hot guys don't stay single long. Take my word for it."

I rolled my eyes. "We're just friends."

She began to walk past me. "If you say so."

In my bedroom, I sank into my bed to think. William liked me, and I liked him, but what could I do with that realization?

Chapter 4

The following day I was back to texting William. The "new" phone worked much better than the refurbished one I had bought online, the one that was stolen.

Any problems with the phone? William texted.

No! You don't know how much helping me out with this means to me, I replied. I sat up on my bed and crossed my legs, eagerly waiting for his response.

It's nothing. It was collecting dust in my drawer at work. You needed it, so I obliged. It lessened the guilt too.

I rocked back and forth, trying to formulate a response in my mind. Giving me the phone may have eased his guilt, but receiving the gift made me feel like a user. Not a good feeling in the least. Maybe it was best to change the subject. *But what could we talk about?* I asked myself. I drummed my fingers across the top of my thigh as I searched for a safe subject. I decided to stick with work.

We had a weird customer at work today, I texted. *Took him twenty minutes to order three donuts. Kept changing his mind.*

I felt extremely lame. As if he'd care about the daily goings-on at the bakery.

Did he at least pick something you made?

No!

Damn! He's really missing out, ya know.

As I went to reply, Harmony's phone number flashed across my screen.

My throat burned. It had been six months since we last spoke and over a year since I had seen her in person. Last I heard, she hadn't paid her rent and was evicted. Lord knew where she was living now *if* she even had a place to stay. The phone rang a few more times before I answered it. I knew how the conversation was likely to go and was half-expecting her to want something.

I exhaled. "Hello?"

Other than the ambient drone of being on the phone, all I could hear were drawn-out, labored breaths.

"What do you want, Harmony?" I asked. A moment ago, I was in a great mood, but she had hit a nerve. "I don't have all day."

"I need your help," Harmony whispered so quietly that I almost couldn't make out what she'd said.

The hair on the back of my neck shot up. I knew it. She needed something from me. Typical.

"What do you want?" The tone of my voice betrayed my exasperation.

"I haven't heard from Mom. Could you maybe call her? She was supposed to call me after Bingo, but of course, she didn't. Maybe she forgot."

I rolled my eyes. "And say what?"

"Tell her to call me, all right?"

Mom probably forgot to call Harmony back and wandered off to go do some shopping or something. She could have been busy rearranging the dishes in her cabinet or maybe she was baking.

"Well, will you?" she prodded when I didn't answer.

"Fine, okay."

Harmony mumbled a weak goodbye and hung up. Not even a "please" or a "thank you." Like Dayton, she only ever called me when she needed something. *Serenity, can you do this? Serenity, [insert problem here]. Serenity, I need you.* I threw my cell on my pillow. Maybe I wouldn't call Mom. My arms tightened. Where were they when I needed them? Whenever I needed a ride or cash or a favor? Of course, they were too busy. Or they had no money. Or they invented lame excuse after lame excuse.

Tears streamed down my face. I was so tired of this. Was this what my relationship with my *family* had been reduced to? We all used one another. Take, take, take. A part of me was guilty of that too, and I often seized what I could get. Maybe not money, but any scrap of attention, any ounce of love; if any of them paid attention to me, I soaked it all up like a sponge.

I picked up the phone again and dialed Mom's number. Whatever Harmony needed from Mom, it must have been important. Those two had an unstable relationship; one minute they acted so damn close, and the next they were strained, awkward. Was it their way of coping maybe? I didn't know.

The number went to voicemail, so I let the phone fall from my mind and switched back to my conversation with William.

When are you off work? Do you still want to hang out? I texted him. Last night, we had made plans to hang out, but we hadn't really confirmed anything.

I'm off at five. Mostly done with everything, but just sitting around until then. I'll pick you up when I'm done.

Okay, I replied.

What would you like to do? William responded.

Maybe he'd invite me to his place. Surely, he had his own

space with no annoying roommates. Some alone time in the comforts of wherever he was living may be what was needed to figure out where we really wanted to go with our budding relationship.

I'm not sure. I was hoping you'd have an idea.

I bit my lip. *Should I suggest his place? Or would that be too intrusive?* I wondered.

Mom's number came across my screen, interrupting any response I was going to type to William. I guess it would have to wait.

I answered the phone. "Hello?"

"Hey, sweetie. Sorry I missed your call."

"It's no problem. Were you busy?"

"I just finished rearranging the furniture in the living room," she said.

"Oh?" I guessed moving couches was close enough to rearranging dishes like she did every week. "So, did you hear from Harmony?"

Mom's tone changed. "Yeah, I told her I'd call her after Bingo. But you know how it is. I got busy, and I lost track of time. I'll call her after I get off the phone with you. Thanks for the reminder, sweetie."

I smiled weakly despite being alone. "No problem, Mom." I rocked back and forth on the bed, anxiously wanting to end the call and respond to William's text. But I had promised myself I'd call Mom when I got a new phone, so I had to fulfill that promise to myself. "So, what are your plans for the rest of the day, Mom?"

"Oh." She paused. "Uh, I may bake another batch of cookies."

Okay, something I could build a conversation on. "Oh, what kind?"

LEAVING THE PIECES BEHIND   49

"Chocolate chip," she said quickly. "Hey, did you ever find another job?"

"Yes, at another bakery."

"That's so wonderful." Mom's voice was cheerful and upbeat. It warmed my heart that I at least I could make her happy. "You learned from the best, you know —"

"I know." I cut Mom off before she could go any further. I knew where this was going. Mom was the best cook I knew back when we had money for food. She taught me how to cook, and she always thought I should have gone to culinary school.

"Things are starting to look up for me, Mom."

"That's good to hear, sweetie. I wish I could help you out more."

"I know, Mom. I love you." I knew she wished things could have turned out differently, but dwelling on the past wouldn't change what happened. At the end of the day, we were taken from her. And then she got us back only to lose us again. She tried. She really did, but it didn't change anything.

"I love you more than you'll ever know, Serenity." There was a sudden crack in her voice. "I better call Harmony. Talk to you again soon."

Click.

And before I was able to say another word, the line went dead.

I gnawed at my fingernail until it bled. Whenever I talked to Mom, old memories resurfaced. I learned at an early age to bury my resentment and accept life for what it was, but it always reared its ugly head sooner or later. The first time we were taken from Mom we had spent a year-and-a-half in foster care. It was a confusing time. Three different homes, three different families with zero people who wanted me. I remembered a few of my fellow foster mates, but for the most part, I blocked nearly everything else. I always just wanted to be back home with my family. Mom took every opportunity to get us back. She attended every supervised visit with a smile on her face. But even back then, I knew she was hurting. How could she not? We weren't with her, and we were her life.

The tears flowed down my cheeks; I couldn't keep them in. She used to tell me she loved me every day. Then the day she got us back, we moved to a little mobile home in a neighboring town. It was a new beginning, but it didn't last. Nothing ever lasted. Twenty-two months later, her sadness took over and...

I stood, unable to think about it any longer. It was over. I couldn't change it, but why couldn't my brain leave it alone? Why couldn't I move on? I paced the room, holding the phone tightly to my chest. My mood dampened with despair, and a gloominess threatened to swallow me whole.

My phone vibrated. I looked down to see William's text floating on the screen.

No ideas either?

I had forgotten I was in the middle of making plans with William. I looked at the message. The big question crossed my mind again. *Decisions, decisions. Should I ask if we should hang out at his place?* I knew he had just gotten out of a long-term relationship, but Crystal's words still rang in my mind. William was a good-looking man. He was almost too good to be true, and so far he'd proven to be a good match for me. He admitted to liking me.

He liked me.

What about your place? I typed. I hung my finger over the

send button and read the message a couple of times, debating whether I should just get it over with.

I heard a knock on the door. *Great, another interruption.* Not wanting to drag it out and have him wondering, I pressed send.

I heard the knocking again. "Serenity?"

I sighed. "What do you want, Sophia?" *Why did she have to be home?*

"Have you seen my hairspray?"

I rolled my eyes. "No!" *That girl loses things faster than she can purchase them*, I thought.

She opened the door and poked her head through. "Are you sure?"

I tried not to roll my eyes again. "Yes, I'm sure."

"So," she said. "Crystal met your new boyfriend, aye?"

I swallowed hard, annoyed. "He's not my boyfriend."

"Then what is he?"

"A friend. And if you don't mind, I was busy making plans."

She was the one to roll her eyes this time. "Whatever. Just let me know if you find my hairspray. I can never find anything in this house."

"Will do."

When she let herself out, I returned to my conversation only to find that there was no reply. Maybe William was thinking or got busy suddenly. Or maybe I shouldn't have said anything in the first place. I had a horrible feeling that I had made him uncomfortable.

Oh, he finally responded fifteen minutes later.

I just thought maybe we could watch a movie or something. Just for a change of scenery, I texted back quickly. I could picture him thinking that I was desperate, and I'd scare him away faster than I could blink. While I wanted to explore our friendship more, I didn't want to force him to do anything he wasn't comfortable with. I didn't like it when people forced things on me after all.

I could take us to a movie theater.

No, I instantly replied. *I have no money to go to a movie. I'm sorry, it was only a suggestion. There are a lot of places we can go to hang out.*

I knew that he meant well, but I wasn't a leech like my mother, my brother, or my sister. I didn't want that label slapped on me. Some of the labels that have been attached to me over the years were true, but some were so false and I had believed them for so long that they still haunted me. I couldn't do it. I would not use William in the slightest way.

My phone vibrated again. *It's no problem, really, Serenity. It's the least I can do.*

Some old umbrage that had nothing to do with William festered in my mind. I couldn't help it. *It matters to me,* I texted back. *I'm not a user. I don't want to use you. Please understand that.*

I couldn't stop shaking. Why was I treating him like this?

Maybe we can make plans another time, he quickly responded.

I didn't want that. I rocked and rocked. I screwed things up already. My body moved in a dull rhythm. What had I done? After Mom's parental rights were taken away for good, I managed to screw up every good thing that had come my way. I'd snap and get mad. Like with William just now. I didn't mean to snap. My message came across wrong. I just wanted him to understand where I was coming from, but now he didn't want to hang out after all.

I lay on the bed, frozen in time. Today had turned to shit, and I couldn't control it. I couldn't control any of this.

Another vibration distracted me from my self-loathing. *I didn't mean to upset you, Serenity. I'm just not used to someone getting upset over a gift or even tickets to a movie. I just want to be able to return the favor.*

I inhaled slowly and let the exhale sooth my frayed nerves. William was a complicated man. I couldn't begin to imagine what was he hoping to gain from this arrangement. He had obviously gravitated toward me for a reason. He may have been kind, but even someone wonderful could have an agenda. What did I have that others didn't? What did he want from me?

But then again, maybe he didn't want anything. Maybe he just wanted to be a knight in shining armor.

Let's not fight. I'll be there in five. Then we can think of something to do that's free. Fair?

I quickly replied, *Sounds good.*

I put the phone down and took another deep breath. I was going to go out and have a good time. I deserved a break from my floundering thoughts and from the painful past that wouldn't stop following me around. I changed into a summer dress, and after debating the idea of make-up for a few moments, I headed for the door.

When I got outside, William was already waiting beside his car. He wore a sharp, pinstripe suit, which instantly put me on edge. Aside from our first few meetings, he typically changed before coming to pick me up, choosing something more casual, more fun. This time he was dressed formally as if he already had a destination in mind and wasn't going to take no for an answer.

"So, where are we going?" I asked tentatively.

He smirked deviously. "You'll see." He halted, noting my hesitation. "Are you coming?"

I nodded meekly. "Yes." The cynicism I felt earlier was returning. Did he not believe me when I told him that I didn't want him to keep doing me favors? This relationship — whatever it was or would become — couldn't be one-sided. Whatever his intentions were, they didn't sit well with me.

When we both got in his car, silence overtook us. I shifted awkwardly in my seat. I didn't want to think this way.

William glowered at me. "What's wrong?"

"I— I don't know," I lied. The words left a bitter taste on my tongue. I hated to lie, but I couldn't help myself. I wanted to tell him the truth. I wanted to tell him why I suddenly felt so self-conscious but couldn't bring myself to do it. *Stupid.*

His expression warmed. "Well, let's go. I just want to show you something."

My shoulders slumped. "Oh, okay. Let's go."

"You had me worried for a second." Once he had his seatbelt on, he turned to look at me. "I've been thinking about what you said, Serenity. I don't want you to feel like you're using me."

I swallowed hard. "I've just been burned a lot of times and don't want to do the same to anyone else."

Tell him about your mother, a little voice said.

No! I answered firmly.

He nodded and looked away.

"What? What is it?" I asked, alarmed.

"I was going to propose coming to pick you up in the mornings and taking you to work. After what happened with those louts, I don't feel like it's safe for you to walk there before sunrise."

I knew he was right. It wasn't safe, and my safety should

be a priority. I wanted to say yes, but then I would only owe him even more.

I could only muster a weak, "I don't know."

William didn't respond as he turned down a street, heading downtown. He pulled into a back alley behind a row of high-rise apartments and guided the car smoothly into a parking spot. I noticed the building was only a few minutes' drive from my house.

"This is what I wanted to show you," he said as he shifted the car into park.

"Where are we?" I asked.

"This is my house," he said. "Want to come in? I need to get changed anyway."

"Okay," I said quickly. My excitement was brewing. *He's inviting me into his house!* He took my suggestion to heart. He really considered what I had to say and here we were at his place. I wondered what it would be like inside.

I followed him around to the front of the building. He retrieved his keys and let us into the lobby. To the right was a modest seating area with a little café. I could see an elevator to the left and a directory mounted above it. First Floor: Highland Dentist. Second Floor: Viker & Johnson Solicitors. Third Floor...

The elevator door opened before I had a chance to finish reading.

"I live on the seventh floor," William said, interrupting my thoughts. "The seventh and eighth floors are residential suites."

I blinked at him, not sure what to say. Instead, I kept my mouth shut as the elevator doors closed in front of us.

On William's floor, we walked down a narrow hallway

with six doors, three on each side. His place was the last room on the right.

After fiddling with the lock, he opened the door and waved me inside. "Here it is!"

The apartment was smaller than I anticipated. There was a tiny kitchen, a dining area, and a living room the size of my bedroom.

"I know it isn't much, but it's close to work and your place," he said, shutting the door behind him.

"At least you have your own space," I said as I looked around. "It's much better than living with roommates."

I took off my shoes and followed him to the back room.

"This is my bedroom," he motioned. "And that door over there is the bathroom if you need to go."

I nodded.

"I'm going to change. Make yourself at home."

I took a seat on his worn leather couch which barely fit in the small space. His place looked well lived in and comfortable; an attribute of home that I hadn't seen in a long time.

He exited his bedroom wearing a long-sleeved t-shirt and blue jeans and sat beside me on the couch.

He scooted over a little so that he was closer to me. "I live so close by, I can just drop you off in the morning." His smile grew, his cheeks rosy and warm. "It's not even out of the way. I drive right by the bakery; why not save you the trip?"

"But don't you start work at 8 AM?"

"Yeah, but I go in early most of the time to catch up on things. On the mornings I do sleep in, I always have a ton of work to take home. So it's really a kick in the ass to me. See, helping you helps me. You know?"

I sniggered. "I guess." And there it was again: the

awkwardness from before.

However, before it could get ahold, he asked, "So? Is that a yes?"

"Yes, I'll let you, William. Come and take me to work so you can get up and be productive in the morning."

He sported a smile that spread from one ear to the other and maybe even a little farther.

"If you put it that way, well, then…"

William leaned in ever so gently. Our mouths interlocked. His lips were soft against mine. His breath had the subtle scent of mint, and my heart skipped a beat. The world around me descended into unfamiliar territory. Time seemed to stand still, whirling me into a merry-go-round of mixed emotions. Then we naturally parted. A wistful smile embraced his lips.

"Tomorrow, 4:30 AM?" he affirmed.

Words did not come easily, and the few that almost made it to my mouth got stuck in my throat. I just nodded while butterflies fluttered wildly in my stomach. *He just kissed me!* I got a glimpse of his smile, yet words failed us both. I wanted to know if this meant we were now more than just friends.

Chapter 5

It had been two weeks since William kissed me and we were still acting like everything was normal. Except it wasn't normal. Everything was strange and transient.

When we pulled up in front of the bakery, William brushed my curly brown hair away from my face, leaned in, and hugged me. "You have a great day, Serenity."

I stared at him and the butterflies in my stomach emerged like they usually did when he touched me. I had feelings for William, yet neither of us had dared to talk about that evening in his apartment. That kiss meant something, but instead of discussing it, we ran with the punches. I wanted something more, and I sensed William wanted the same. What was holding us back? I wanted to ask him if we were still just friends, or if we were a couple, or if it was something in-between. Had we reached that awkward past-being-friends-but-not-quite-in-a-relationship stage yet? It was all so confusing.

"You have a great day too. Call you later."

I stepped out of the car and toward the door of the bakery. William stared at me and smiled before driving away. I stared at the taillights as they faded in the distance. When was I going to tell him how I felt?

"What are you thinking about?" Zina asked, holding the door open for me.

I turned and looked at her. "Nothing." I managed a weak smile before following her into the bakery.

"Ya thinking about that young hunk?"

I nodded. "A little." I couldn't keep the smile from my face.

"Why don't you get on already and tell me what's on ya mind? I do know one thing or another about relationships."

In the back room, I took my time getting ready. A knot formed in my throat. I wasn't sure at all what to say; Zina would definitely think my dilemma was childish. It was *so* middle school. Girls worrying about petty things like if a guy liked her or not. I was an adult, and asking William if we were together or not shouldn't have felt like some big, bad thing. I paced the little room for a few moments before I went to start my shift. Zina stood beside me at the large table, rolling her dough as I prepared my own.

"So, what is on your mind?" she asked finally.

"Nothing. It's not important."

Zina chuckled. "Don't you tell me it's nothin'. I always hated it when my daughter used to say that, especially when 'nothing' was always code for something. Don't discount your troubles as nothing. I'm always here to listen. I don't judge."

I took a deep breath. "William, the boss's friend, and I have been seeing each other — sorta — for a while."

Zina stopped rolling her dough and glared at me. "And?"

I shifted nervously. "Well, we kissed." I looked away, my face growing hot.

Zina chuckled again. "No reason to be embarrassed. That's a good thing, isn't it?"

I reluctantly turned to look at her. "I guess. Except it hasn't happened since, and I don't know if it meant anything, or if it was a mistake." Everything tumbled out at once, and I wasn't sure if I wanted it to or not.

Zina stopped what she was doing and placed her hand on my shoulder. "Do you think it was a mistake?"

"No."

"Have you asked William how it made him feel?"

I shook my head. "That's the problem: I don't know how to ask. I just don't know how to approach it. I'm also afraid of rejection."

Zina glanced at me sympathetically. "I know how ya feel. I remember back in the day when I met my husband. I was a timid girl. I knew he liked me, and I think he knew I liked him. We spent a good few months talking, going out to the movies with our group of friends. We even hung out a few times — alone — before I gathered the courage to ask him if we could be exclusive. Turns out he was worried about the same things. He didn't know if I would want to date him." Zina paused, clearly reflecting on her youth. "I guess my point is, sometimes you just gotta go for it. If he continues to want to hang out with you, it's likely he's just as nervous." She patted my shoulder once more before returning to work.

I turned and focused on the task at hand. My mind was floundering again. I knew Zina was right. No man I had ever dated before wanted to spend as much time with me as William did. No man had ever offered to drive me to work in the morning. And why would William invite me back to his place if he didn't like me? Was he just as reserved as I was? A part of me wondered if inviting me to his house was a huge step for him. Well, if he wasn't going to bring up the status of our relationship, maybe I had to.

"Thanks for the advice, Zina. I'm going to do it."

"That a girl," she said with a wide grin.

I finished another tray of dinner rolls and brought them over to the oven. After talking with Zina, I felt better, more at peace about my feelings. Mom used to tell me that life was too short to stress even though she stressed every day. Zina reminded me of my mother though she was more like the mother I wished I had. I loved my mother, but I so wished I could call her and tell her all about William and ask for her advice about what I should do. Instead, I shared my greatest fears with Zina, a work acquaintance. My throat itched, and I had to strain to keep myself from crying. One day I would have that kind of relationship with Mom.

I would make it happen.

Soon six o'clock rolled around and the rest of the morning staff appeared right on schedule. Like every day, the tranquil environment turned into a battleground, and my mind spun at a million miles per hour.

"Pass me the sugar, Serenity."

When I didn't react, there was a tap on my shoulder.

"Pass the sugar already."

I jumped and quickly passed it along. "Sorry," I whispered.

My heart skipped in an unfamiliar way. I had better not let my petty problems get in the way of my job. So far I had been doing well and didn't want to get on anyone's bad side, especially when my life was just turning around.

I spent the majority of my remaining shift in silence, doing what I needed to do without communicating with any of the other bakers. Not that it mattered. I didn't click with anyone besides Zina anyway. Some of them even treated me as if I was continually encroaching into their territory. At least when I worked for *George's Bakery*, I got along well with most of the other bakers. We were all in our late-teens and early-twenties, so it made sense. Here, I was one of the youngest employees, and it showed.

Once one o'clock rolled around, Zina and I left the bakery.

"So, what is your plan for this afternoon?" she asked casually as we stepped out into the sunshine.

"I'm heading home," I told her. I had an entire day planned with me, myself, and some solitaire. Maybe even thinking about William between games. "What about you?"

"Would you like to grab a cup of coffee? I don't have anything planned this afternoon."

I stood there dumbfounded for a minute.

"Unless you're busy," she said quickly.

"No, coffee sounds good." It was way better than chilling with Sophia and dealing with whatever drama she had for the day.

"How about the coffee shop down the street?" she suggested.

I nodded. "Sure."

I followed Zina down the street. My hand was cupped in my pocket where I had a few bills left over from my last paycheck. We entered the coffee shop. I was pretty sure we had delivered pastries to this place a few times. The decor was dated, and the floors were covered in scuff marks from years of wear-and-tear, but otherwise it was a quaint spot. And it smelled and looked clean, which was always a plus.

A young man approached the till. "What can I get you ladies today?"

Zina ordered a coffee, and I ordered a hot chocolate.

Once we received our drinks, we made our way to a corner table and I sat across from her.

She sipped her coffee. "I just wanted to see how you're

doing."

"Oh?" I replied. I didn't know what else to say.

"Nothing bad, dear," she clarified. "I've seen how that hunk looks at you."

I blushed. "I don't know. It's complicated."

Zina took another sip and laughed. "It's only as complicated as you make it. So practice on me. What do you want to tell him? Now, don't be shy."

"Well..." My mind spun around like a spinning top. I couldn't believe I was sharing all this with Zina. "I want to know if we're officially dating or not. We talk every day and hang out a lot. I enjoy his company and I know he enjoys mine. I want to put a label on what we have. I can't explain it. I don't even like labels, but in this instance, I do. I need it." I wanted to slam my head into the ground like a cartoon ostrich; I could only imagine how scatter-brained I sounded.

"Take a deep breath," Zina advised.

Great, she noticed too. I did as she instructed.

She smiled. "Good."

"Sorry," I mumbled.

"Don't be, Serenity. Don't be," she replied. "Now, about your dilemma. How would you feel about setting up a fun little date? Maybe some activity that you both can enjoy. Then casually bring up the state of your relationship. Like maybe a walk or bowling? Something where the two of you are interacting and talking. No movies," she added.

I sat there for a moment, soaking in what she was saying.

Wanting to avoid looking clueless, I murmured a quick, "Thanks." Maybe she was right. I could ask William if he wanted to go to bowling or take a walk around the mall. Then I could pick the perfect moment to blurt out what I needed to say.

My phone rang. It was my mom.

Taking her cue, Zina stood up. "I'm going to run to the bathroom real quick. Don't worry about me," she said and scurried away. She probably assumed it was William.

I connected. "Hello, Mom."

"Hey, Serenity. How are you doing?"

"I'm fine. I'm just having coffee with a co-worker. How are you?"

There was an awkward pause. "I won't keep you..."

"No, it's fine. She's using the restroom, so I have a minute or two."

There was an obnoxious tapping on the other line. Mom's nerves were acting up most likely. "I just wanted to see if you'd be busy next weekend. I'm going to be in town looking at some houses."

That piqued my attention. "Houses?"

I heard some labored breathing on the other line. "Yeah, Mike," she continued. "You remember Mike, right?"

His name sounded familiar. "I think so." I thought back to my childhood and could barely conjure up a face. I decided that he must have been around when we came back to live with Mom.

"Well, anyway, the landlord sold the house, so we're moving. I thought maybe to where you live. It seems nice, and maybe we could spend more time together. Would you like that?" She sounded hopeful.

Zina returned from the bathroom and sat down.

"That would be nice." I felt a twinge of guilt. "Can I call you back later, Mom?"

Mom's voice trailed off. "Oh... Okay, sweetie. You take care." *Click.*

Zina stared at me sympathetically. "Is everything all right?"

I smiled. "Yes, that was just my mom. She's going to be in town next weekend."

"That's nice."

The pain my chest festered. I knew I should be excited that Mom was coming to visit, but it made me a bit distressed. It made me want to crawl into a little ball in a dark hole somewhere. I wouldn't tell Zina that though.

I looked at the time. It was shortly after two, and I needed to head home soon.

Zina finished the last of her drink while I had barely touched my own. "You seem preoccupied," she said. "Is there somewhere you need to be?"

I swallowed hard. "No," I lied. What I really needed was to make plans with William as soon as possible. I wanted to get it all out. I wanted to finally clear things up between us. But ending this meeting abruptly would be rude.

Zina was wise enough, though, to pick up on the subtle cues that I must have been giving off. "Well, I'd better get going. I'm sure you and William will be meeting up later."

"Have a great evening. I'll see you at work."

"Same." She smiled before she headed for the door.

She was right. William was on my mind, but so was my mother. I would have to call her back sometime before she came to town.

After Zina left the coffee shop, I sat for a few moments, debating what I was going to do next. William wasn't off work until five, and I wasn't sure if he had any other plans tonight. Neither of us had mentioned anything before.

What are you up to? I typed.

My fingers could barely finish a coherent thought. I really wanted to see him. In the back of my head, a million ideas stirred, but none took hold. What would we do? Maybe I could dress up and look real nice. Mix things up and throw him off his game but in a good way. Then once we were relaxed and his walls were down, I'd ask him if we were officially dating.

The plan was perfect in theory, but my nerves were another story. Could I pull it off?

I just finished with a client. I have a few minutes. How was work?

I smiled. *It was pretty good. I went for coffee with a co-worker. Now I'm about to head home. Are you available to hang out tonight?*

I tapped my foot against the booth, my slender legs trembling. *Please be available. Please*, I kept telling myself. If there was ever a moment that we needed to meet, tonight was the night. Zina finally gave me the kick in the arse I needed.

I was about to ask you the same thing. I'll be off in an hour. Short day today.

I was in the middle of typing a response when he texted again.

Pick you up at your house.

I deleted my original response and replied, *Okay, sounds good.*

I quickly left the coffee shop, passing Zina who was just boarding the bus. I picked up the pace past the area where I was robbed. Even the twinge of fear that had attached itself to the location didn't stop me. I was both nervous and excited to see William and finally, *finally* have some answers.

Inside my house, I wasted no time hopping into the shower. I wanted to look my best when William picked me up.

I changed into a purple cocktail dress; I had bought it on clearance a few years ago and had rarely worn it, but tonight seemed like a great occasion.

I bounced out of my bedroom toward the living room, skirting right past Sophia.

She stopped and stared. "Someone is in a good mood." There was a hint of passive-aggressiveness in her voice, but at that very moment, I couldn't care less.

I sat on the couch and waited. I kept glancing out the window and then back to my phone. I couldn't stop fidgeting. Finally, at quarter-after-four, William's car pulled up in front of my home. Sophia had entered the living room.

"Do I look all right?" I asked her nervously.

Sophia nodded. "I don't think I've ever seen you dress up to that extent before if I'm honest."

I took her somewhat rude comment as a yes and let myself out of the house. Not waiting for William, I opened the passenger door and slid inside.

William smiled, his eyes wide. "You look pretty. Are we going somewhere?"

I shrugged. "No real plans."

"Could we maybe stop and get some delicious treats before the bakery closes? I've been thinking about you all day, and what better way to kick off the night than to eat one of those delicious cinnamon buns?"

I started to nod, then a different idea popped in my head. "I have a better idea."

He rose his eyebrow. "Oh?"

"Instead of buying them, why don't we make them?"

This was perfect. Zina said to plan a fun activity. Not only could we do something fun, but maybe we could also bond over something.

"I'm not a great baker," he tried to reason.

"But I am. Trust me, we can make better cinnamon buns."

He licked his lips. "So, what do we need?"

"We can make a quick stop at the grocery store."

"Okay. Let's go. Then we can go back to my place and make them. It's a little more private and all. Right?"

"Right."

William pulled away and headed toward the local shop. *So far so good*, I kept telling myself.

He pulled into the parking lot. "How about here?"

"Sure." Normally, I would have bussed across town to the cheaper market, but I didn't want to remind him of my money troubles.

As we strolled down the aisles looking for the list of ingredients, William stared in awe like a child in a toy store. It warmed my heart. It was rare to see such delight, and I wasn't accustomed to it.

"Is everything all right?" William finally asked.

"Huh?"

"The pretty dress, the shopping, and all that stuff. It just caught me off-guard, but in a good way."

"I just wanted to look nice for you."

William blushed.

"We got everything," I said, eager to change the subject. I reached into my pocket. All of this would take most of what I had left. I sighed. But I needed to resolve this dilemma today.

William shifted foot-to-foot the entire time we were at the till.

The cashier shot off the total, and I reached into my pocket for my money, but William handed the lady his credit card.

I mumbled a thank you.

Inside the car, I sat quietly. I wanted to pay for it, but once again, William had me beat.

William touched my shoulder. I jumped. "Don't feel bad about me picking up the tab. It's just a habit, and besides, you're going to teach me your mad baking skills. It's the least I can do."

"Maybe I will." If he only knew of my mad baking skills. If he *only* knew.

At his apartment, I unloaded the ingredients onto his small counter, rearranging items nervously so we'd have ample workspace. Droplets of perspiration dotted my forehead.

William stared at the counter. "Where do we begin?"

"Do you have a large mixing bowl?" I prayed that he did. I didn't think to ask before starting this whole charade.

He pointed to his top drawer. "All my dishes are up there, and underneath are my cooking utensils."

I pulled out a large mixing bowl and a cookie sheet. I smiled. "First, we mix in the dry ingredients." I measured and dumped the contents into the bowl.

William stood there looking on in amazement, taking in everything I was saying. I handed him a spoon. "You stir while I add in the liquids."

He mixed, and I cracked an egg into the bowl. "Now, I'm going to mix in the milk slowly. It's going to get a little difficult to stir in a bit, but it'll start to take shape."

The dough was taking form, and William was excited. Even I was excited.

"Now we let it rise for a bit." I laid a towel over the bowl and washed my hands before walking into his living room. William followed.

"You do it with such ease," William complimented as we sat side-by-side on the couch.

"Just like you make numbers easy, yeah?"

William rubbed his neck. "Not nearly as exciting as being able to bake."

I shuffled over so our legs touched. His left hand touched my knee, but we maintained eye contact. I reached over and kissed him. This time, I would make the first move. William pulled away after a second and his eyes widened, his posture stiffening for a moment before he relaxed. I must have caught him off-guard. That seemed to be the theme of tonight. But then he reached over, cupping my chin and pulling me closer as our lips touched again. We stayed entangled for a moment, and then pulled away. It felt right. Natural. Despite the kiss, we didn't say anything. We didn't have to.

My phone rang. *Oh, God. Why didn't I turn it off?*

Groaning, I pulled it out to stare at the screen.

"Sorry, it's my mom"

"Why don't you take it?" William said.

When I turned to answer the phone, I swore I heard William sigh with relief.

"Hello," I said.

"Hey, Serenity. Sorry our last conversation got cut short."

I placed my elbow on my knee and rested my head in my hand. "It's all good."

"What are you up to?"

"I'm just hanging out with my boy— my friend. I'm hanging out with my friend." I didn't bother to make eye contact with William. My face burned.

"Oh!" Mom exclaimed.

"We are baking," I clarified before she could ask anything embarrassing. I rocked back and forth; my heart was pounding. I didn't mean to blurt that out. I mean, I planned on asking William first. This just wasn't how I imagined bringing it up.

"That's nice," she replied. She paused for a moment before continuing. "I'm for sure coming next weekend. Maybe I can meet your boyfriend then."

"My friend, and yes. Maybe. I don't know. We'll see." I kept stumbling on my thoughts.

"I won't keep you. Call me when you aren't busy, okay, sweetie?"

"Okay, Mom."

"I love you."

I took a deep breath. "I love you too, Mom. Talk to you later." Then the phone clicked.

I slowly put the phone back into my pocket and forced myself to look over at William. He didn't say anything.

I guess now was a better time than any. "That is what I wanted to talk to you about."

"About?" His words were shaky. I think he knew what I was referring to, but he was too nervous to admit it.

Here it comes…

"Are we dating?" I asked. "Or what?"

William's gaze averted from mine.

Crap. "Sorry," I mumbled.

William then turned to look at me. "Do you want to be my girlfriend?"

"I do." As soon as I said it, I felt a weight lift off my shoulders.

He smiled. "Then I guess neither of one of us has to guess

anymore."

I pulled him close to me, almost too roughly, and kissed him. Warmth radiated throughout my body, and my heartbeat raced. William grinned cheek to cheek. I never wanted that moment to end.

It was official.

We were a couple.

Chapter 6

I'll be in town later this afternoon. Where do you want to meet?

I reread the text from Mom. The pit in my throat tightened. She told me she was coming, but I guess I just didn't believe it. I paced, my mind floundering with thoughts of how this meeting was going to go.

How about we meet at a little café near my house? I suggested.

A sudden sadness hampered my heart. I wanted a better relationship with Mom. I told myself, I told her, and I even told Dayton before he ditched town that I wanted to see more of Mom. I had formulated a plan in my mind to see her more often. But now she was coming in a few short hours to see me. Why was I so sad? Why was I dreading seeing my mother?

Then Mom's number crossed my caller display.

I reluctantly answered. "Hello?"

"Hey, sweetie." Mom's voice was cheerful. I heard a distinct male voice in the background. More than likely it was Mike, the one she said she was going to bring with her when we last spoke.

"Hey, Mom."

"We are about ten minutes from the city. Where do you live? We can come to pick you up."

My throat tickled. "Okay." I shot off my address to her. *What am I doing?* Regret, or a sense of dismay, invaded my thoughts. I almost wanted to make up an excuse not to see her. What was wrong with me? My childhood wasn't so bad that I deserved to feel this way about my mother. So why now?

"Is everything all right?" Mom asked.

"Sorry," I mumbled. "I just have a lot on my mind from work."

"You were always a hard worker," Mom responded.

"Thanks. I'm going to go shower real quick. Text me when you're here."

"Okay, see you soon. I love you."

"I love you too, Mom."

I lay back on my bed and stared at the ceiling. I didn't need to shower. It was a lie. A little white lie. The little ones I had always used when I was on the brink of being overwhelmed.

What are you doing? I texted William.

I'm doing some paperwork for work on Monday. It's been a busy week, he responded a few minutes later.

I'll message you later. I have to get ready to meet my Mom soon anyway.

I put my phone down and strolled over to my dresser. Last Christmas Mom knitted me a sweater. Mom had a real knack for knitting. She had a lot of talent — wasted talent, but talent nonetheless. It was sad. I hoped that today was a good day for her.

I waited for ten minutes and expected Mom to show up. Then another ten minutes went by. Then another. An hour passed before her text came. I left through the door into the living room. Sophia had her nose in a book when I approached.

"Some car is outside. Is that for you?" she asked.

"Yeah, just my mom."

"Oh! Why don't you invite her in?" Sophia asked.

"She wants to take me out to eat."

Sophia shrugged and went back to her book.

Mom's old rusted car sat out front. I remembered that car back when we were returned to her the first time. I didn't know she still had it. All of the other times we had met up, she was driving a different car. I thought this red car was long gone.

Mom got out of the passenger seat. She was wearing a black silk blouse and a navy pair of slacks. She had makeup on, and her curly red hair was tamed. She smiled, radiating warmth. I smiled back. For the first time, I felt maybe this meeting would turn out okay.

She strolled toward me with open arms. I wrapped my arms around her tightly.

"I missed you," she said.

"I missed you too, Mom."

When we pulled away, she glanced at me and smiled. "Is that the sweater I made you?"

"Yes." I smiled back. She recognized my efforts.

"We better get going. Mike is starving."

I got into the back seat.

"Hello, Serenity," Mike said. My vague memories of Mike came rushing back. I met Mike a few weeks before I turned ten. It was the first weekend back living with Mom. She told me things were going to be different starting with a new car. Ironically the same car I was sitting in now. The new house, new beds, and even new toys. Mom had gone all out when Dayton, Harmony, and I came home. She was happy then.

"Hi," I responded sheepishly. I swore at myself. *Don't screw up today, Serenity.* Mom was happy, and I didn't want to ruin things.

"So where are we heading to eat?" Mike responded, rubbing his big belly.

"There is a little diner a few blocks away," I suggested.

"Okay."

I shot him the address, and he punched it into his phone and drove away from the curb.

"How have you been?" Mom asked.

"Working a lot. Dealing with annoying roommates and…" *Did I want to tell her about William?*

"And?" Mom prompted. "Is something wrong?"

"No!" My face grew hot. Little butterflies invaded my thoughts.

The car came to an abrupt stop. "I don't know about you ladies, but I'm starving."

"Me too," Mom said.

I got out of the car and a sudden relief washed over me. Right now wasn't the time to bring up William. Mom would want to meet him, and I wasn't ready to spring my Mom onto William yet.

Mom followed me into the diner.

Mike found a seat by the window and Mom sat beside him while I sat on the other side of the table.

A perky waitress approached us with a few menus. "Can I get you anything to drink?"

"Water," I said.

Mom ordered the same. Mike ordered an extra-large milkshake. If I remembered Mike from when I was a child, I think he was the type of person who just had to order the biggest of everything. We'd see if my memory served me well and I hadn't mixed him up with any of the other "special friends" Mom had.

"It's so nice to see you, sweetie," Mom interrupted my musings. "I've been looking forward to seeing you for a while."

"Me too. It's been way too long. So, what have you been up to you?"

"Mike might have a new job in the next town over. Wouldn't that be nice?" she asked him.

Mike nodded. "Yup, and good pay too. And don't forget to mention the houses we're going to look at. That little sum of money you received will sure help."

His comment rubbed me the wrong way. I couldn't pinpoint why. "That's nice to hear."

"It'll be a new beginning," Mom said.

I tried so hard not to roll my eyes. Mom's new beginnings never lasted. I wondered what happened this time that caused her to uproot what life she had and move out here.

"Is everything all right?" I asked.

Mom sighed. "There are no jobs back home. Mike was laid off, and I lost the job I did have. You know how it is."

I reached over and touched Mom's hand. She flinched. "You look great, Mom. I'm glad for your new beginning. Things will get better. They always do."

She grinned as the waitress returned with our drinks.

"Are you ready to order?" she asked.

"I am," Mike chimed in. "Not sure about these ladies. Too busy chitchatting."

The waitress didn't say anything.

"I'm ready," Mom said.

I glared at her for a moment. She had never been here before and didn't even so much as glanced at the menu.

"What can I get for you?" the waitress prompted.

Mike spoke first. "Two double cheeseburgers with a lot of mayo. I mean *a lot* of mayo."

"And you?" The waitress turned to me.

"Chicken Caesar wrap, with french fries." It was a staple item at this café and the only thing I'd order.

The waitress stared at my mother who sat there silently. Mom's face reddened. She hastily said she wasn't ready from the pressure.

I saw Mike roll his eyes. "Hurry up and order, Melody," he said.

Mom glanced down at her lap.

"They have great Denver sandwiches here," I suggested.

"I— I'll get that," Mom stammered.

I glared at Mike who simply shrugged and slurped down more of his milkshake. At that moment, I wanted to reach over the table and dump it on him. But I didn't. I wouldn't embarrass Mom further. She'd probably just end up defending him anyway. It was obvious he had no problem making her feel small. I didn't remember him ever being this mean, this callous. But I didn't really remember a lot about him anyway because they broke up shortly before they took us from her again.

Mom frowned, and what little positive glow she had before disappeared completely.

"I can't believe you still have that car." I said, trying to change the subject. A trip down memory lane would either cheer her up or make her more depressed. It was a risk worth taking with nothing to lose really.

Mom smiled. "I was afraid you wouldn't remember."

Mike rolled his eyes yet again. "She would've been better off spending the money on a new car than fixing up that rust bucket."

"It runs doesn't it?" I snapped. I was seething. The negativity dripping from him was nauseating, and it took every ounce of my being not to tell him to fuck off. I turned my focus back to Mom. "So where was it stored all this time?"

"It doesn't matter," she said quietly.

"It matters to me. I remember that car, and I remember the first drive-in movie in that car. I remember when Harmony nearly gave you a heart attack when she stuck half her body out the window."

"Yeah, that girl would never sit down." A small smile formed across her face. If Mike would shut up with the comments, then maybe I could still salvage this meeting.

"It's nice to see it running again," I said, attempting to lighten my tone and forget about Mike being there.

Mom's tone changed too. She seemed to become more comfortable and confident. "I had looked at other cars, but I decided to pay a friend to put a new transmission in. It runs like a dream. I hoped you'd recognize it. You and Harmony always fought over who got the front seat."

I bit my lip. Harmony usually got her way when we were kids.

"Have you talked to Harmony lately?" Mom asked.

I shook my head. "Not really. She isn't online anymore, and I haven't talked to her since she called me."

Mom sighed. "I was hoping you had heard from her. Her phone got disconnected a few weeks ago, and I haven't had much luck getting a hold of her."

The waitress brought us our food, and we sat in silence for a few minutes.

"I do hope she is doing all right," Mom finally said.

Mike scoffed. "I'm sure she is doing fine, Melody. Give

her some time. You worry too much."

I narrowed my eyes and crossed my arms. I had to keep telling myself to chill and not let him get to me. Mom chose to be with him, and that also meant that she was choosing to let him treat her with disrespect.

"I'm sure she is," she said quietly. "You're right."

Mike's chin jutted out like a snake as he shoved the greasy burger into his mouth. He wiped his face with his sleeve. He was so gross. He squinted at me with a dismissive glance. I returned an equally intense stare. How much I wished he'd just go away and let Mom and me be.

"Melody," he said, not bothering to cover his mouth or finish chewing before speaking.

"Yes, hun."

"On our way back, we should look at other cities for rentals. You know, keep our options open."

I tapped my foot. It was taking every ounce of restraint for me to not react. If Mom was the one to be spending her money on this move, then she should have the last say.

"I'll be right back, Mom. I need to use the washroom."

I stood and strolled toward the bathroom. Suppressing my feelings was something I always had to do, so I was used to it now. Inside the bathroom stall, I sat on the toilet seat and sighed.

I checked my phone messages. There was a text from William: *I hope you're having a great time with your mom.*

I wish she didn't bring her 'boyfriend.' He's an ass. I threw a few angry face emoticons in there before sending.

Oh? he responded a few moments later.

He's just so rude. I'd hate to see how he treats her when I'm not around. I'm just in the bathroom taking a few moments before I join them again. Thanks for listening and I'll text you tonight.

I held the phone to my chest and took a deep breath. *Just don't overreact*, I told myself. I didn't want to make things worse for Mom when she did leave. Whether or not she did move here, I wanted to make the best of this visit because it may be my last with her for a long while.

Call me if you need a ride, William replied.

I will.

Without waiting for a response from him, I returned to the table.

Mom and Mike stopped talking when I sat back down.

"Are you almost done eating?" Mom asked me. "I really need to go back to our motel."

"Why?" I asked.

She looked away. "Mike's tired."

"Then he can go sleep, and we can go to the mall or something," I suggested. I didn't even care about how rude I was being. All I knew is that some much-needed time with my mom without him would be wonderful.

"I don't know..." Her voice trailed off. Mike didn't seem to be bothered by where this conversation was heading.

"How often do you spend time with me?"

"I know." She turned to look at Mike. "What do you think?"

I kept my mouth shut. Why was she asking him for permission to hang out with her daughter? Better yet, why was she putting me second again and again?

"Do what you want, Melody, but you might have to find your ride back if I don't wake up."

Mom looked downward.

"I can make sure you get back to the motel," I offered. I'd personally take the bus with her to wherever she was staying if I had to. I just wanted her to choose me. I wanted her to *want* to spend time with me. I just really wanted to know how she was doing without him. Deep down, I had this overwhelming feeling that this would be the last time I'd see Mom for a long time.

"Well," Mike interjected. "I'm done eating, so I'm going to go. Call me later, and maybe I'll come to pick you up." He reached over and kissed my mom on the forehead before heading out the café door.

When he was out of sight, Mom let out a sigh of relief.

"How are you doing really?" I asked.

Mom smiled. "He is a great guy."

"I didn't say he wasn't, Mom."

Mom frowned. "I could tell you didn't like him."

"I think the feelings were mutual. But it doesn't matter. If you love him, Mom, then that is all that matters."

Mom's eyes darted around the large room. "It'd be nice to have all you kids together in the same room."

"One day soon, Mom. Try not to think about it."

"It would be a miracle. I can't even get Dayton to return any of my emails. He doesn't want to see me. I wonder how he is…"

I gulped, hoping and praying she didn't ask me about him.

"Have you heard from him lately?" she finally asked.

Shit!

"It's been a while," I said sadly.

"Why? Is he okay? Please be honest with me if you know anything."

"He's in jail." I frowned. "I had bailed him out of jail, then he went on the run and got arrested again."

Mom wrapped her arms around herself. "What did he

do?"

"This last time he stole a car. I only found out from a news article."

Tears emerged in Mom's eyes. "It's all my fault. He always blamed me for everything. He is right. I was a shitty mother."

"It's not your fault, Mom." That familiar bitter taste in my mouth returned. "He made his own choices, and he has to face the consequences. He's an adult now."

Mom didn't say anything.

"You are a good mom," I said. "None of what happened... none of what *is* happening is your fault. Please, stop blaming yourself."

I had my share of resentment and issues with Mom, but now wasn't the time to bring them up. She felt bad enough. She didn't need me to kick her when she was already feeling down.

"I couldn't keep it together for you kids." Her self-doubt talk was seeping out.

I reached over and held her hand. "It's a new beginning. You said you wanted to move here for a new start. It can be better. Whatever happened in the past is in the past. Right?"

"You're right." She lifted her head. "You were always so insightful. Such a smart, beautiful person. You know that, Serenity?"

I smiled. "I got it from you."

I never knew my father, so someone had to get the credit. Mom had terrific qualities underneath all the layers of problems, but depression was a severe thing.

"At least you didn't inherit the negative qualities," she joked.

I chuckled. "I'm well-balanced."

We both laughed at my lame joke.

"What else is new with you, sweetie?" she asked again. "Besides work. Anyone special?"

I hesitated, which was all the evidence she needed.

"Who is he?" Mom said.

"I started seeing this guy, William. It's not too serious."

"What do you mean 'not too serious'? Do you mean not-living-together-serious?"

"I mean not serious." I was unsure if I wanted to give her more information. "We only just became official. And kissed a handful of times. It's pretty innocent."

"At least you are taking things slow. Harmony seems like she has a new boyfriend every week. I can't keep track."

I shrugged. "I'm not Harmony."

"If things get serious, you'll introduce me to this William?"

"Of course."

It wasn't a complete lie. I didn't want to introduce William to *anyone* until I was sure he was the real deal. Our relationship was already complicated enough without presenting him to Mom.

Mom took the last bite of her sandwich. "How about we head out," she suggested.

She paid for our meal and we exited the restaurant, walking toward the center of downtown. "There is a mall a few blocks down," I began. "You can see it from here. It's the tall brick building."

Mom nodded. "Okay, let's go."

We crossed the street to the corner where I was robbed that fateful night. The bakery was just a block over from the usual way to the mall. "Do you want to see where I work,

Mom?" I asked.

"Sure. I like to know what is happening in your life."

As we walked closer to the exact point where I was jumped, my heart sped up, anxiety naturally propelling me forward at a break-neck pace. Mom had to jog to keep up, but I couldn't help it. Every time I approached that spot since that night, I get goosebumps and feel uncontrollable fear. What if they came back? I couldn't afford to lose any more of my stuff. While I had a job, it still wasn't enough to save much. Here I was hoping for a raise or promotion soon. One day I'd hopefully get my own place and with it total freedom from Sophia and Crystal and all the juvenile drama that followed. Maybe then William would come over. But it was wishful thinking. Every single dream I formulated was out of reach. A shitty reality.

Mom stopped to catch her breath. "What was *that*?" she asked.

"Nothing," I lied quickly. *Think, Serenity, think!*

"Where are we?" she asked, looking at the building in front of her.

I walked up to the front of work. "This is where I work. It's closed unfortunately, otherwise I'd show you inside."

Mom nodded. "Cute little place. Have you ever thought about opening your own bakery?"

I nodded. "It has crossed my mind. Just everything costs money. Which isn't easy to come by."

A gleam formed in Mom's eye. "It's a worthwhile goal. Dream big. You have so much potential, sweetie. I always believed you could do big things. You did well in school despite... well, your upbringing. You graduated, you're working and have so much ambition. I couldn't be prouder of you." She touched my arm gently.

"Thanks, Mom." I paused. "Shall we keep going?"

A playful grin spread across her face. Mom took large carefree steps as she followed me. We arrived in front of the mall where she took a seat on a nearby bench. "Let's sit."

I did as she asked.

"It's such a beautiful day, Serenity. Why not enjoy it?" Her mood seemed to be picking up now that Mike wasn't with us which just reinforced my dislike of the guy.

"Okay."

"I remember when you were first born. You were such an easy-going baby. I could take you to the malls and people would stop and tell me what a beautiful baby you were. They'd comment on your curly, dark-brown hair and your cute little dimples. You were truly perfect, Serenity. Everywhere you went, you lit up the room with your charm. Now I look at you, all beautiful."

My face grew hot. Mom was experiencing what I considered a positive high. She expressed so much joy. I soaked it up. But I knew it would come to an end, it was just a matter of when.

"As soon as Dayton deals with his legal problems," she continued. "And Harmony finally contacts me, I'm going to make it my mission to get all my kids together."

I smiled. I wasn't sure Dayton would be open to that idea. The picture-perfect meeting that Mom was imagining wasn't going to go her way. But I had to go along with it for her sake.

Then Mom's phone rang.

She stared at the phone and ushered me to be quiet.

"Hello?"

Her expression dropped and the smile she had a moment ago faded.

"I'm just at the mall with Serenity. Do you need me now?"

She did some nodding and her mouth twisted in a frown. I heard Mike's voice on the other line. What did he want?

After a few minutes, she hung up the phone.

"I'm sorry, my girl. I need to go."

My posture stooped. "Why? I thought we were having a good day."

She hesitated before speaking. "We were, I mean we are. But Mike is distraught. He wants to leave early tomorrow and doesn't want to sleep alone."

I drew my limbs close to me. "But why?"

Mom slumped. "He's on his way to pick me up."

I stared down at my feet. She was going to go through with this. She was going to choose him over her me, her daughter.

"I don't get to see you very often." I could feel my bottom lip start to quiver. I just wanted to spend time with my mom. We were having such a great day.

"It'll be different soon, I promise."

I didn't say anything as Mom's car pulled up a few minutes later and she headed for the passenger seat.

"Don't go, Mom." I tried to hide my sniffle.

Mike rolled down the window. "Will you hurry up, Melody? I don't got all day."

I stood straighter. "What is your problem?" I approached the window. Mom tried to stop me, but I shrugged her away. "What is so damn important that she has to leave right now just because you say so?"

Mike waved his hand dismissively. "Back up. This isn't any of your concern."

I turned to look at Mom. "You're going to ditch me?"

"I'll call you later, I promise."

"Just like you promised to spend the day with me?"

Mom looked downward. "Don't be mad, Serenity."

"Don't be mad? You are abandoning me! You are deserting me all over again. You don't need to go with him. You can stay here. We can get our own place, and I can help with the rent. We can rebuild our relationship. Don't you want that, Mom?"

The car honked.

My chin trembled. "Mom?"

"Will you hurry up?" Mike prodded again.

Mom covered her face with her hands. "I— I got to go, Serenity. I love you."

She turned and ran to the passenger door. The door shut and Mike drove off. I slumped into the bench, and I cried. Why couldn't she, for once, choose me?

I   wanted   my   mom.

Chapter 7

After work was done on Monday, William's house was the first place I went to. If I couldn't go to my boyfriend for comfort, what did I have?

When I got into his car, he asked, "How are you?"

I forced eye contact and tears threatened to fall for the billionth time since Saturday. Sunday sucked, and work today sucked even more with the reminder of Mom lingering. "I've been better."

He reached over and kissed me. "Maybe when we get to my house, I can make you feel better."

"I hope so."

On the way to William's house, I stared out the window at nothing in particular. I was in a slump. My shoulders drooped and the corners my mouth followed. I wasn't sure why William wanted to hang out with me. *I* wouldn't hang out with me. I was depressing to be around. A piece of me felt numb, almost like it had been ripped away from me.

We arrived at his place. Before exiting the vehicle, I looked at my phone messages again. I had a bunch of missed calls from Mom.

Inside the apartment, I cuddled with William on the couch. My phone rang again, but I wasn't ready to talk to Mom yet. The bitterness from the other day left a lot to be desired. She had sent me a dozen or so text messages and had called me close to twenty times. Every time she failed to keep her word, she always did this. I was so sick of her broken promises.

"Are you all right?" William asked as he held me.

I sighed. "I will be." I faked a smile and looked into his eyes. A warm feeling formed in my chest. I could count on William. He hadn't screwed me over yet.

"I know things didn't go well with your Mom. Are you sure you don't want to talk about it?" William asked.

I shook my head. I wasn't ready to tell him about Mom just yet. That wall was firmly in place protecting my heart and keeping my vulnerabilities at bay. William seemed to be the same way. He hadn't shared much about his past either. For the time being, this approach worked for us.

He placed a small kiss on my forehead. "I understand." His eyes danced a little, sending a wave of ease through me. He was so reassuring, and I appreciated it.

"Thanks," I whispered.

He reached behind me to retrieve the remote and turned on the television. "Maybe we can find something to watch."

I nodded. "I'm cool with anything."

My phone vibrated again, and against my better judgment, I checked it.

I love you. I know you're mad. We need to talk about this. I hated to leave you like that. Talk soon. xoxo Mom.

I shoved my phone back into my pocket. *Then why did she leave me there if she hated to see me like that?* I asked myself, but I already knew the answer. She chose him over me like she did time and time again. She loved me, but she couldn't put me first. She couldn't keep her promises no matter how hard she tried.

I stood up from the couch. "I need to use the bathroom."

I scooted past where William sat and made my way to his bathroom. I closed the door and stared into the small rustic mirror on the wall. My eyeliner had started to run at the sides. I took a piece of toilet paper and dabbed the edges of my eyes to prevent the raccoon-look from taking effect.

I stared into the mirror and let my mind wander. If only William knew what was going on in my mind. To get out all these thoughts, all of these damn disappointments, and get my anxiety-filled mind games out into the open would be a huge relief even if he couldn't relate. I couldn't be the only one in the world with a mother who couldn't keep her promises.

There was a knock on the door. "Are you all right in there?" William asked.

"Coming." I threw the soiled paper away and made my way out of the door.

William had returned to the couch. I strolled over to him and nearly plopped myself in his lap as I stared intensely into his eyes. "Do you know how handsome I think you are?"

He blushed.

"I mean it." I wanted to take the focus off of myself for a moment. Selfish, I realized, but I wanted one moment not to think about my problems.

He smiled then reached over and kissed me. "Thanks, you too."

I giggled. We were lame, but I loved it.

He bit his lip. "I'm here for you, Serenity. I know we haven't known each other that long, but I really do care about you. Ever since I picked you up from visiting your mom, I've been worried about you. I just want you to know that."

The extreme pressure of the moment weighed down my

heart. A voice in my head was pushing me to tell him about what happened. To tell him about how much of an ass Mike was and how he screwed up everything with Mom even though Mom was at fault too. I wanted it not to be her fault. Then maybe it wouldn't hurt so much.

William sat there without saying a word. He didn't have to. I assumed he could read me.

He averted his gaze, his eyes darting around the room.

"I appreciate it. I really do, William." My vulnerabilities were clashing. *Just open up already, Serenity, God dammit!* The two sides swirling in my brain couldn't come to a compromise. "I'm just scared. Not of you, but of life. It hasn't been kind to me. You understand?"

William smoothed the front of his shirt with his left hand. He cleared his throat. "I understand." He took a deep breath. "A little too much." He forced a smile. "My relationship with my parents hasn't always been easy. I kind of get the sense — but I could be wrong — that you're also estranged from your family. I don't mean to intrude..." He paused to catch his breath and opened his mouth to speak again but stopped.

A twinge of guilt and apprehension tugged at my gut. *But why? We had something in common.* The only thing I could do was force myself to open up a little. Let him in a little bit. How could we be in a relationship if I continued to close myself off from him?

"I grew up in foster care," I blurted out. I glanced down at the floor for a moment before I forced myself to reconnect with his gaze. "That was how I spent nearly half of my childhood before I aged out." Eight years in total. It was longer for both Harmony and Dayton.

He nodded sympathetically. "I spent a year in care. My parents were both addicts, but my dad got it together and got custody of my sister and me."

I managed a weak smile, reached over, and hugged him. He understood where I came from. The relief was so palpable that I could feel the weight lift off my chest. I wondered if William had jumped from home to home even during the short time he was away from his family.

"I'm happy that you got reunited with your father," I said.

"Thanks, me too," he said. "So how is your relationship with your dad?"

I sucked in a breath but didn't say anything.

"Not good?" He frowned. "Sorry."

I shrugged. "I can't say either way. I've never met my biological father. My mother never talks about him. All I know is that she says I'm better off without him." I grew up always wondering about him. The few people I got the courage to ask, like my Aunt Jane, told me he was bad news and was never meant to be a father. But as it turned out neither was my mother ready to be a mother.

"Oh!"

"It's fine," I went on. "You can't really miss something you never had." For a long time, I did feel like I was missing something. But after a while, it really didn't matter as much. Regaining a meaningful relationship with Mom weighed on me more than wanting to find my father. It was odd: after all the ups and downs and turmoil, I still wanted that close mother-daughter relationship.

"Maybe we can locate your father," William suggested then looked away just as quickly. "Sorry, not my place."

"It's fine." I placed my hand on his thigh. "I know you mean well. I think we both need to stop saying sorry or feeling nervous or whatever seems to be holding us back from just saying what's on our minds." The relief of the situation cleared the dead presence around us. It was freeing. "I'm tired of worrying about saying the wrong thing, worrying about if you're going to reject me and run away from my life. I just want to take a risk."

I stood up from where we sat and paced. The small area seemed to instantly open up just like my newfound perspective. A total one-eighty from how I felt before. "I just haven't met someone like you." For some reason, this was all spilling out of me. William didn't say anything. "Someone with so many layers, so many great qualities. Someone I feel like I could connect with." My mind was flying at a million miles per-hour.

He didn't move. He appeared to be thinking.

"I didn't mean to put you on the spot, honestly." I took that as my cue to sit back down.

He wrapped his arm around me. "When I first saw you at *George's*, you looked familiar." He stopped to catch his breath. "Then when I ran into you that one day and you told me your name, I remembered where I met you. I was fourteen, and I think you were around nine, but we spent a few months with Susan, I think her name was. We weren't super close, but it was just nice to reconnect with someone from that dark time in my life. I just…"

A lightbulb turned on in my head. It was no wonder that I felt so comfortable around him; I already knew him in some way. I tried to remember 14-year-old William but couldn't conjure anything. Regardless, I found comfort in his words. He was like me.

I waited a moment for him to finish, but he stopped abruptly. "You just?" I prompted.

"I was just afraid to tell you, I guess," he whispered. "My ex-girlfriend left me high and dry when she found out I was a foster kid. It was like it was some deep, dark secret, a plague to our relationship. It was like I was too *broken* for her. I guess I was afraid that if I told you where I remembered you from, you'd run away."

I stared deeply into his eyes, half-confused, half-intrigued at his assessment. "I don't understand. I'm a foster kid as well. Why did you think I'd run away?"

He glanced behind me, avoiding eye contact. "I— I don't know." He chuckled. "Assuming the worst, I guess. I just thought you'd want to leave any trace of that life behind. That I'd be a constant reminder. When I lived with my dad, I spent most of my time isolated at home studying. There was a determination to make a life for myself.

"Growing up, my mom had this expectation of me. When I first reconnected with her after I turned eighteen, one conversation we had, she told me she wanted me to break the cycle. *'Go to school, get a good-paying job, and make me proud.'* When I lived with her, she expected me to do well at everything. When she couldn't get up in the morning or would lock herself in her room and cry at night, I was expected to keep the household going. "

"And you accomplished just that," I said.

William gazed at me. His eyes sparkled, almost smiling. "Do you remember when I took you by that campus on our first unofficial date?"

I smiled even though the painful memory of that night was etched in my brain. "Yes."

"When you asked me if I attended that school and I said 'no.' The true reason was that that was where my mom and dad met. They were two people who should have never gotten together. They were toxic together. It was part of the reason why I chose not to attend the university. But I wish I would have."

I caressed his cheek. "I understand. We all made choices we wish we could change now. But look on the bright side, we wouldn't have reconnected if we took different paths, right?"

William nodded in agreement but remained silent.

I had spent years reliving my earlier memories and years more trying to repress a lot of them. For the first few weeks in care, I blamed myself for us kids being taken away. I tried to replay what I could have done differently. I would have reminded Mom to do the laundry or go grocery shopping more often. She was busy with other things. But I knew that wasn't the case. She was just too depressed to get out of bed. Deep down inside, I thought I knew it, but I was only eight. We painted this picture-perfect image in our minds — I know I did — that everything was fine. Even now I still hoped things would get better.

"Would you like to go for a walk?" William asked. "I need some air."

I nodded.

William stood from the couch and rushed to the door. He had always been a chill kind of guy, but right now he was on edge.

He locked up behind us on our way out. The tensions were high despite the realization that we came from the same cloth.

Chapter 8

I spent the next few days looking through my limited belongings from my stints in the foster system. I couldn't believe William remembered me, but I wanted to remember him. What he looked like, how he acted, something he said. Anything really. I was searching for something from that time that would be able to piece together what he was like or at least what I was like. I had lived through so many changes and in so many homes that my memories, both good and bad, were jumbled.

I found one photo album and flipped through it, hoping to find anything relating to William. Most of the photos were of my brother, sister, and me from the times when we could visit one another. I could never stay with them. The adults always told me that since I was the oldest, I needed to be brave for my brother and sister. It was a kick in the ass to be honest.

My phone vibrated again. If it wasn't for the possibility of William messaging me, I'd have just shut it off altogether.

I'll make it up to you.

I heaved labored breaths in and out. *Couldn't she take a hint?* I didn't want to talk to her. She couldn't make it up to me. She couldn't keep a promise if her life depended on it. I tried to believe her, and this last time I thought there was a small chance she'd keep her word. But she didn't.

A bitter taste filled in my mouth. Instead, she ditched me to go with that jerk. My fists clenched. As much as I hated the guy, at the end of the day, Mom was an adult who made her own decisions. And she decided to ditch me.

I closed the photo album, threw my phone beside it, and left the room. I needed a breather. Sophia was sitting on the couch watching television. She had already taken all her finals last week and was bound to be a pain in my ass until fall classes started.

"What are you up to?" she asked. "You've been spending a lot of time in your room."

I shrugged and sat beside her. "Been busy."

"Busy doing what?" She flipped the channel. "Busy laying on your bed talking to your *boyfriend?*"

I shrugged again. "Partly." It wasn't a lie. I had been spending a lot of time texting William, but he was at work for another hour.

"I don't know why it has to be a deep dark secret," Sophia replied. "Besides, maybe I can offer you some advice."

I laughed. "Advice? What can you advise me on?" She and her college boyfriend, Andy… Anthony — I couldn't even remember the guy's name — had been dating for a bit, so maybe that *qualified* her to give me dating advice.

She frowned for a moment and crossed her arms. "Never mind."

I was amused, but I fought back a smile. "No, really, I want to hear your advice."

Sophia stood up to walk away, but stopped and glared at me before saying, "Don't let your guard down."

I shook my head. "I never let my guard down."

"I mean it." She had her hands on her hips.

I sighed. "Things are going well between us. So I'm not

going to overthink anything if that's what you mean about not letting my guard down."

I tried to keep an open mind. Unlike me, Sophia never had to jump around, waiting for the next bomb to drop. When something good came my way, it was freeing to let my barriers down even if it was terrifying to take that leap.

"Andre hurt me so much," she continued.

Her eyes were jaded, and I felt a little sorry for her. Under it all, that attitude illustrated a girl with genuine feelings.

Andre, that was his name! And who would have guessed? I thought.

"Some men just suck," I said softly.

She bit her lip. "But he can be so nice at the same time." Her face was contorted, confused perhaps.

"Does he call you names?" Before William and I became a thing, I was on the receiving end of some pretty terrible verbal abuse from an ex. Fat, worthless, stupid—the list went on. I told her as much.

"Sometimes." She sat down. "I never told anyone this, but I caught him cheating on me with my sister."

I opened my mouth to respond but stopped. I couldn't imagine Harmony sleeping with my boyfriend, but it wouldn't be a surprise necessarily. She was always envious of what I had.

I finally managed to find my words. "You know, you don't have to stay with him." After seeing how Mike treated my mother, I didn't wish that kind of treatment on anyone. Even Sophia.

She bit her lip and looked away.

The most surprising thing was that this was a side of Sophia that I didn't realize existed. It was a layer that I didn't think was possible. She was always so annoying and rude, but maybe she had the same barriers I did.

"I know. My point is, don't let your guard down. I'm not saying it'll happen to you, but men are pigs." Her sorrow turned to anger as she stood up and marched into the kitchen, leaving the remote behind.

I debated changing the channel but decided against it. Sooner or later, William would text me, and we'd likely make plans to meet up and do something. I headed down the hall and back to my bedroom to think. On my bed, my phone lit up. My heart rate sped up, and I became giddy. There was one text from Mom and one from William from about ten minutes ago that read, *I'm off work in half an hour. I'm wondering if you'd like to come over. I have something I want to show you.*

Yesterday he was busy with work stuff, and he promised we'd hang out today. William always kept his promises. I didn't care what Sophia had to say. I didn't need to keep my guard up around William. But I wondered what it was that he had to show me. Ever since our breakthrough, I'd felt at ease. Now all that weight was lifted, and I felt like I could be myself and enjoy learning all I could about William.

I can't wait. After entering a few emoticons, I sent him the quick response before sprawling on my bed and staring up at the popcorn ceiling. A smile crossed my face at the realization of how happy he made me. I felt blessed.

In my puzzled mind, I kept trying to imagine what he wanted to show me. I wasn't one for surprises, but William was an exception. He showed me his home, he made me his girlfriend, and he had shown me repeatedly that he genuinely liked me. So what else could he show me?

Then the doorbell rang. I jumped from my bed and

sprinted out of the room to the front door. Of course Sophia was already there, and William stood there and smiled when our eyes connected. She turned, winked at me, and walked away.

I hugged him and planted a soft kiss on his lips.

He blushed before handing me a rose. "I got this for you." I poked myself on the thorn on the stem. "Pain is beauty, I was once told," he said with a wince.

"Thanks," I replied, sucking my thumb. I reached over, and we kissed again. "I'm going to put this in some water, and I'll be right out." My heart tingled. He nodded, and we parted as he walked outside.

I rushed into the kitchen for a glass, filled it with water, and placed the rose in it. I set it on the window ledge above the kitchen sink.

"That's pretty," Sophia said from the entryway.

"Thanks." I hurried past her. "I wish I could stay and chat, but I got plans."

"Have fun."

"Thanks."

Without another word, I rushed outside. Only William's car was nowhere to be found. "William?" I whispered.

He stood near the bushes that spread onto the sidewalk. "Are you ready?"

"Yeah!" I looked around.

"I thought maybe we could go for a walk. I left my car at home and walked to work this morning. I've been cooped up inside these past few days with work. I thought maybe some fresh air would be nice."

"Yeah." I didn't care what we did as long as I got to spend the day with him. He held out his hand which I happily took. "Where we headed?"

"My place. I have something to show you, remember?"

I thought the rose was my surprise, yet he had something more to show me. My body filled with glee. I couldn't wait to find out what he had in store. Every time we hung out, there was always something new to explore.

We walked until we came to the main road. It was still rush hour, and this happened to be one of the busiest intersections on this side of the city.

William held on to my hand as traffic swooshed by. He caressed my palm, shooting warmth throughout my entire body. His place was still a few blocks away and in the opposite direction from where I worked.

When the street cleared, we crossed, still holding hands. Butterflies fluttered in my chest, all giddy like a girl who had a crush on the cutest boy in English class. But instead this was real life, and William was my boyfriend. Even being exclusive, the title *boyfriend* still made me grin cheek-to-cheek.

"Not much farther," William announced, distracting my line of thought. Not that I minded.

I nestled my head into his shoulder, and he responded by stopping us in the middle of the sidewalk and gently kissing me on the forehead.

When we finally reached William's place, I made myself at home on his sofa.

He wandered into the small kitchen. "Would you like anything to drink?" he asked.

"Some water, please and thank you."

He brought the glass to me and sat on the edge of the couch. "How was your day?"

I took a sip. "It was pretty decent. I managed to finish an order for a wedding. I had to ice two-hundred-and-fifty cupcakes."

"Did you save one for me?" William asked hopefully.

I lightly ran my finger across his chin. "Unfortunately not."

"Darn." He frowned before smiling again. "On a serious note, before I forget, I'll be right back."

He rose from the chair and headed for his bedroom. I heard him rummaging around a bit before he returned to the living room with a shoe box and sat it on the coffee table in front of us.

"What is that?" I asked.

He opened the lid. "This is what I wanted to show you. After we opened up to one another, I did some digging and found some old photos from the foster home we both stayed in. I wanted to share some with you."

He took out a small stack of photos and leaned back against the couch. I laid my head against him.

The first photo was of a young boy sitting with my foster mother Susan in her knee-high socks. She liked her socks.

William spoke. "This is Anthony. I don't know if you remember him, but he came around the same time I did." William glared at the photo for a moment. "I remember the night they dropped him off. He cried for hours. We shared a room with two others, and finally the only way he'd fall asleep was when I told him a story."

I felt so lucky to be with William right now. Even during a dark moment in our lives — when his own life was so full of uncertainty — he showed compassion for another.

William turned to another photo. This one I instantly recognized as William.

I held it in my palm, examining it. "You were cute, even

back then." I beamed at him. That photo was of a boy who was tall and lanky and wearing blue-striped pajama pants. The best part about it was that I began to remember him.

He smiled and changed to another photo. "Not as cute as this girl."

A tear formed in my eye. It was a picture of me sitting on the front porch of that house. I remembered when this took place. Susan had taken a bunch of us kids on a walk to the park a few blocks away. It was one of the only things I looked forward to back then. I stared at the younger version of myself. My hair was tied back into mismatched pigtails, and I was wearing a black-and-white polka-dotted spring dress that was swimming on me.

"Where did you find these?" I asked, not looking up from the photo.

"When I turned eighteen, I located Susan and asked her if she had anything from the time I stayed with her. This shoebox was the only thing she had left. It was some pictures and a few small gifts my parents had sent me that I had never taken with me. Apparently she kept all of them over the years even after we left."

I managed to fake a smile. While I was happy for him to be able to collect these moments, on the inside a sudden sadness formed. I had never returned to any of the many foster homes I had lived in to gather any memories I had left behind. I had a few photos and gifts that were given to me back then, but I never held onto most of the stuff I had owned from my childhood for one reason or another.

William put the photos back in the box and closed the lid. "I'm sorry."

"For?"

He hugged me. "I can see it on your face, that sadness. I

thought showing you those photos would make you happy and hopefully bring back some good memories."

I sighed and looked at him. "Don't be sorry. I appreciate you showing me them. I recognize you now that I have seen the photo, and I'm so glad you told me the story about Anthony."

He patted my shoulder. "But it brought up some unresolved feelings, hasn't it?"

I nodded. "Yeah, it did." I paused to catch my breath. "I just look back and I wish now that I would have thought of locating my previous foster parents. Even if it is just for closure."

"It's not too late."

I breathed in deeply and exhaled. "I wouldn't even know where to start."

William pulled me closer. "I can help you. If you want to find your prior foster parents, then I want to help you."

I shook my head. "I can't expect that much from you."

"Why?" he asked. "Is it really that hard for you to accept others' help?"

I pulled away from him. "No!"

"I *want* to help you. I want you to find peace."

I didn't respond. The guilt festered again. William had already been there for me so much, especially after my latest visit with Mom. How could I expect him to keep helping me?

"What are you afraid of?" he asked.

"I don't like using people."

"Is it using when it's coming from someone who loves you?"

My brain froze like a water droplet in the middle of February. "W — what?"

William bit his lip. "I said, I love you."

So my mind wasn't playing tricks on me.

"I'm sorry if that is sudden or too soon," he said quickly when I didn't respond. "But I can't ignore this feeling."

My mind kept spinning. *He loves me. Me.* We had been a couple for a while, long enough by today's standards.

"I'm sorry..." he started to say.

"Stop saying sorry," I interrupted. "I was just surprised. I didn't expect it."

William looked away.

I touched his thigh gently. "I care about you, and I have strong feelings for you, but I don't want to say those three words just because it's expected," I added. I wanted to pound my head against the wall as if I couldn't make this moment even more painful, more awkward for him.

William averted his eyes. "I understand. I know you care about me. I just expected a different response." He looked back up at me with wide eyes and hugged me.

I mumbled a weak apology.

"How about we order a pizza or something? Are you hungry?" he offered.

I nodded.

"Then if you're up to it, maybe we can cuddle and watch a movie?"

I nodded again. "I'd love that."

Chapter 9

Zina stood beside me as we prepared the day's food. My heart felt heavy. I didn't want to be there. The smell of cinnamon lingered in my hair, and I was repulsed by it. I couldn't get it out even after my shower.

"What's on your mind?" Zina asked.

I glanced at her as tears threatened to emerge in waves. "Just been a shitty few days."

When I woke up for work that morning, I noticed Mom had texted me around three in the morning. *I give up. I won't call you again.* Those words stung me to my core. She was giving up. A mixture of bitterness and defeat lingered.

"Do you want to talk about it?" Zina asked.

I looked away and rolled the dough. "She keeps abandoning me." I sucked in a deep breath. "And William told me he loved me and I didn't say it back." That thought jumped out of my head, out of nowhere. It had been on my mind too, of course. But I had been trying to suppress it and pretend he never told me.

Zina put her hand on my shoulder. "Take a deep breath, Serenity."

I stopped and did as she said. I inhaled and exhaled a few times, regaining my composure.

"Now tell me who abandoned you." Zina returned to her task.

"My mother." I repeatedly played the events of the day over in my mind. "I hadn't seen her in a while. She and her boyfriend came to see me. We were having a good day until she abandoned me again."

I thought ignoring my Mom's texts and calls would make me feel better, but when she finally stopped attempting to message me, I folded. Even when I kept my distance, she still found a way to hurt me. She always ripped my guts out, tearing my soul apart with every decision she made. One moment she could be patient and admit she was wrong, but somehow she would make me feel like shit again.

Zina didn't say a word.

"I'm sorry," I whispered as I turned to focus back on the task at hand. I couldn't let my personal life interfere with my job. The last thing I needed was to end up on the unemployment line again. That was one part of my life that I had regained some control over.

"Would you like to take the rest of the day off?" Zina asked. "You seem like you need a break."

I shook my head. "I need the money." I bit my lip and wiped away the few tear droplets that had fallen down my cheeks and got back to work. "I will shake it off and work. I do need the money."

Zina nodded. "That's the spirit."

One day of pay was easily sixty-five dollars after taxes. That was equal to my bus pass for a full month. The only thing that taking a "me day" would do is cause more stress since I would lack the funds for one more bill.

We worked in silence. I was too afraid to speak, too afraid of crying again. Zina had noted my feelings. If I wasn't careful, my vulnerability would get me fired. Opening up to William had been a relief, but lowering these walls around

Zina opened another can of worms altogether. That wasn't her fault.

I focused on my hands and the work that they seemed to be completing without my brain. My mind kept running in circles, threatening to explode at any moment. I needed to keep my cool. Zina liked me well enough, but even she would have her limits. I didn't want to let William down either.

I shoved the pan into the oven and caught my hand on the burner. I pulled my hand away, sucking on the injury. I swore under my breath.

After a few moments, I returned the counter, ignoring the angry throbbing coming from my hand. I needed to keep it together.

"Serenity!"

I jumped.

"Could you pass me the butter?"

I stared at Zina like a foreign object for a moment before handing her the butter.

She smiled. "Thanks, Serenity."

I smiled weakly back and turned back to my task, my heartbeat still racing. I was jumpy.

"Everyone has bad days," she said finally.

I turned to look at her.

"I can see it," she said. "I didn't want to say anything, but I want you to know you've been heard."

"Thanks," I replied meekly.

"Today I'm going to keep you on preparation instead of till. Then hopefully tomorrow will be a better day."

I tried to object, but Zina walked over and placed her hand on my shoulder.

"I'm sorry about your mom, and I'm sorry about your

relationship problems with William. I'm sorry you feel abandoned. I understand."

I formed a half-grin. "I'm trying not to let it show."

Zina replied. "I'll give you my number and after work hours, feel free to contact me at any time if you need to talk."

My spirit lifted a little. Instead of reprimanding me or telling me to suck it up like I'd heard from others, she offered to help. Even if it was just a listening ear, it was nice.

"Thanks so much. You don't know how much that means."

"Now take a few deep breaths and let's get this order done before the six o'clock shift gets here."

I nodded.

The dread weighing on my chest began to evaporate. All I needed to do was get through the shift. I could go home and relax, text William, and text Zina.

Soon the next shift arrived. I kept to myself like I did most mornings. I managed to finish what I needed to.

"Ginni, you'll be on till today," Zina said.

"What?" He stared at her for a moment.

"I'm changing things up today. You'll be on till. Serenity and Lee will be preparing the bread for the weekly school order, and the rest of us will prepare the soup kitchen order."

Ginni grumbled something but complied.

After we got our assignments, I switched stations which was now on the opposite side from where I normally worked beside Lee. He was an older man probably in his late-forties, short, and he spoke broken English. He was quiet but nice enough.

He pointed to a large bowl. "I already add the flour. You take it from here. Okay?"

I nodded. I pulled out the recipe for the white bread. It

had been a while since I made it. A little refresher was needed. I scanned the ingredients and instructions.

"We need to get these rising quickly," he said.

I nodded. "Once I do a few, the others will fly right by."

Lee grinned and said nothing more.

After the first two batches, I finally got the hang of it. The change of pace and the lack of a sickeningly sweet scent was amazing. I thought about the different kinds of bread I could make. Whole wheat, rye, swiss bread. I wondered if William would like homemade bread. He loved the donuts and cinnamon buns I made. Maybe that was what I would do for our next date: I'd buy the ingredients on my next payday and make him some homemade bread. It didn't take a lot to make him happy, and the way to his heart was definitely through his stomach. He loved food. I started thinking about what else I could make, maybe a stew with some whole wheat dinner rolls to accompany it.

The remainder of my morning flew by without a hitch. When one o'clock finally rolled around, Zina and I ditched work.

"Are you in a better mood?" Zina asked me as she stood several feet away from the front door.

"Yeah." While a little lingering sadness swirled around me, I had managed to pacify myself. "It just had been a rough few days. I'm not emotional like that. I just don't know what came over me." A part of me appreciated her concern, but I was embarrassed nonetheless. I didn't want to look weak. Weakness was what people prayed on, took advantage of. But not Zina. Besides William, Zina was the second person who I had been able to be vulnerable with in a long, long time.

"Why don't we take a walk?" she suggested.

I nodded. "All right."

We walked in the direction of my home.

Zina broke the silence first. "I'm all ears if you want to talk. You mentioned something about your mother?"

A dark cloud swarm over me again. "I hadn't seen her in months. She lives in another state. We talked occasionally on the phone."

"It must be hard not seeing her often, correct?"

I glanced away for a second before making eye contact with Zina once again. "It's complicated." Mom and I were like same sides of two magnets: always repelling from one another. We tried, and no matter what our relationship was shitty.

"She..." I trailed off. I wasn't sure what to say to Zina about my mother. Lately, Zina had contained all the qualities I wished Mom had.

"I was estranged with my mother right up to her death last year." Zina frowned for a moment.

"I'm sorry." No other words felt right to say. It was the truth, and I understood it. "I've been estranged from my own mother for years. I've tried to reconnect with her but she keeps letting me down."

Zina placed her hand on my shoulder, a sign of reassurement, at least for me. "Sometimes we just have to lower our expectations. I don't know your situation, but for me I tried to force some kind of bond with my own mother that just wasn't there. She was always distant. When she got sick and went to the hospital, I visited her. I sat with her. During her moments of consciousness, we just sat and stared at one another. I read the morning paper to her. It was the staple of her morning routine. I put our differences aside and accepted things for what they were." Zina stopped in front of a chain-link fence. "You're so young, Serenity. You remind me so much of my daughter. Smart, kind, and so full of love."

I smiled. "Thanks." My body filled with warmth. "Thanks for the pep talk. It was what I needed."

Zina chuckled. "Now that you're smiling, how are you and William doing?"

My shoulders slumped. "All right. But I think I made a mistake."

"Now, now. I'm sure it's not too bad."

"He told me he loved me, and I couldn't say it back. I froze." I let out a labored breath. "I care about him. But he looked so sad. We haven't texted as much lately."

"You didn't make a mistake, love."

"Then why does it feel like I did?"

"No one is saying you don't care about him. No one is saying you don't have feelings for him. Those three little words are a big deal. The time will come when you will say them and mean them."

I nodded. I had been thinking about that night over and over again. The rejection he must have felt injected me with so much guilt. I shouldn't have felt guilty, but I did. He was a good guy — the best I ever had — but I wasn't ready. I wasn't ready to say those damn words. Those damn three little words. So many times when I told someone I loved them, they stabbed me in the back. They took advantage of me.

But William was different. Maybe it was time to break the last piece of the barrier guarding my heart.

"Thanks, Zina. I just need to stop overthinking it. I overthink every little thing instead of just accepting things as they are. I need to accept things as they are, and I need to accept my relationship as it is."

Zina smiled but didn't say anything. *Letting go,* I thought. I had to let go. I had to accept Mom wasn't capable of being there for me. I had to accept that I wouldn't have the kind of relationship with Dayton and Harmony as I pictured in my head growing up. All those kids I used to envy who went home with their parents, walking with their siblings all smiles. I never had that with my family and it was time to accept that I never will.

"Here, Serenity." Zina handed me a piece of paper. "My number. Text me anytime. I have to run some errands. Talk to you tomorrow?"

"Talk to you tomorrow."

Zina headed for the bus stop as I made my way back toward my house. When I reached the front steps, I stopped and sat down on the stoop. I pulled out my cell.

What are you doing tonight? I texted William.

Not much! he texted back a few minutes later.

I was thinking about you.

Me too. I smiled at the heart emoticon he sent along with it.

I sat for a few more minutes on the steps and enjoyed the refreshing air before heading inside. I flopped down on my bed, remembering the conversation I had with Zina. She was right. I put too much thought into expectations. I pulled out my phone and re-read the text my mom sent me that morning: *I give up. I won't call you again.*

She had been attempting to apologize, but I wouldn't let her in. I couldn't force her to be there for me any more than I could force a relationship with her.

I accept things for what they are, Mom.

I didn't expect a response.

My phone vibrated again. Another text from William.

*Finally, I get a free moment. Today has been hectic. How was yours?
I can't wait to see you.*

I smiled. *I look forward to it. XOXO*

XOXO, he texted back.

I turned on my side and texted the number Zina gave me.
Any good recipes for great dinner rolls?

Chapter 10

I lay on my bed texting William, like I did every morning on my day off, when there was a knock on the door. "Serenity."

I exhaled a breath. "What?" Even after getting to know Sophia on a more personal level she still had a way of bothering me.

"Someone's at the door for you."

"William?" I asked.

"No. He didn't say who he was, but he told me to tell you it's urgent."

Without responding, I dragged myself out of bed. Maybe those few calls from unknown numbers I've been receiving the past few days were from the same person standing at my front door.

I swiftly walked down the hallway. *Who could it be?* I wasn't expecting anyone, and Sophia said "he." When I reached the front door, Sophia stood by staring at me, her old nosy self. Eventually she ambled away but was still snooping within my sight. I walked outside.

Outside by the tree "he" stood. My heart sped up. "What are you doing here?"

My brother Dayton turned to stare at me. My lip curled, and my face grew hot. It took every ounce of my being not to yell.

"Hey, Serenity." His voice was low and uncertain.

I wouldn't fall for his sob-story this time. "What do you want? And why aren't you still in jail? Who bailed you out this time?"

Dayton shrugged. "No one."

"Are you sure you didn't guilt Mom into bailing you out?"

I backed away from him with a shudder.

Dayton frowned. "Yeah, as if she'd ever bail me out. She was never there for us then and she sure as hell wouldn't be there for me now." He mumbled something else, but I couldn't hear, nor did I care. I stood there at a loss for words.

"Then how did you get out of jail?" I asked. "Are you on the run? Didn't you steal a car or something?" I looked up and down the street expecting to see some run-down piece idling by the curb.

He pulled at his collar. "How did you know?"

I shook my head. "Why does it matter?" I glanced away, choking on the overwhelming anger forming inside me. Dayton tried to walk toward me, but I backed away farther. "Stop. Why are you here? What do you want?"

"I need your help."

My heartbeat was pounding out of my chest. Not literally, but pretty damn close. "Fuck off."

I turned to head back to the house. I didn't have time for this. I had no time for him. He was a leech, and he'd never change. He'd never fucking change. He'd keep taking and taking and taking until he bled me dry. Then he'd toss me aside as he did before.

He caught up and tapped me on the shoulder. "Serenity, wait. Please."

I nudged him off and proceeded inside, slamming the

door behind me.

"Who was that?" Sophia demanded.

"Nobody."

I sighed and headed back to my bedroom. I had no time for his drama. I didn't know how Dayton had managed to get himself out of jail or whose phone he was using to call me, but I wanted no part of any of it. If he came to apologize or pay back the money he owed me, I'd entertain his stupid drama *maybe*. Just the thought — the audacity of him asking me for money — who did he think he was?

I picked up my phone as a way to distract my roiling mind.

There was a text from William. *What are you up too?*

I pondered burdening him with my problems with my brother. I did mention to William briefly about how my brother ditched town after I bailed him out of jail. Dayton's level of entitlement made me seethe.

My brother showed up, and I told him to leave.

More like I didn't give him a choice, I thought but didn't text.

Isn't he in jail? William replied.

That is what I thought. But he's out. How I don't know. But I don't want to see him right now. I took a deep breath and shot him another text before he could respond. *Do you want to catch a movie or something? I really wouldn't mind getting out of this house.*

He quickly replied, *I just finished up with some paperwork for work on Monday and was about to ask you if you wanted to hang out. I'll stop by right now, if you're ready.*

I am ready. XoXo

Okay, see you soon.

I shoved my phone in my pocket. Knowing Dayton, he'd be relentless and try to come back to harass me some more, only I wouldn't be here if he tried. Maybe today would be the day I spent the night at William's. We came close to a sleepover before, but it just never happened for one reason or another.

I was determined that I wouldn't let Dayton ruin my day. I had little extra money left over from last week's check, and I intended to have a good day with William. He and I were like two peas in a pod. Things had smoothed over, and after my talk with Zina life had been so freeing. At least until today. Free-loading brothers didn't help the case.

Entering the living room, I plopped down beside Sophia. "If he comes back, tell him I'm not home."

Sophia stared at me. "He's still out there."

I took a deep, laboured breath. "Doesn't he take a fucking hint?"

"Who is he?"

I exhaled again. "My brother."

"You really don't get along with your family, do you?"

I wanted to tell her to mind her own business, but I didn't. It wasn't her fault my family sucked. "We're estranged. And my brother only ever comes along when he needs something."

"Did you tell him to leave?"

I shrugged. "He's relentless. But luckily, I won't be around soon to deal with him. So if he gives you any troubles, just call the police." I stood and stretched.

She eyed me. "Where are you going?"

I managed a smile. "William and I are going to a movie."

Sophia smirked. "Is that all?" She winked.

"Maybe. Maybe not."

Sophia glanced out the window. "You're boyfriend is

here."

I turned to stand. "I'll talk to you later."

"How are you going to get out there without confronting your brother?" she asked as I made my way to the door.

That was a good question. *Do I wait until William comes to the door, or do I just run out there, hop in the car, and tell him to drive?*

Before I could worry about it anymore, Sophia answered my question. "Well, looks like William is getting out his car."

"Shit! I better go."

She stared at me sympathetically. "Have a good day."

"You too."

The doorbell rang, and I quickly answered it.

"Hey." He smiled.

I hugged him, and we kissed. "Ready?" My limbs shook a little.

"Are you all right?"

"Yeah," I whispered. "But turns out my brother hasn't left and is lurking."

"Is he the one wearing all blue?"

I nodded.

He held my hand. "We'll make a break for it."

I closed the door just as Dayton came from the neighbor's front lawn and walked to our front porch. "Serenity," he said but stopped cold when William and I stepped onto the grass. He stared at William, brushing his hand through his shaggy brown hair. "Who's this?"

"Never mind. Don't you have someone else you can harass?" I took William's hand and urged him to keep walking.

William obliged without saying a word.

"What is your problem, Serenity?" Dayton asked. "I said I

was sorry."

I stopped in my tracks and turned toward my brother. "You never apologized to anyone in your entire life. Now go."

William wrapped his arm around my shoulders.

"What is this? Is this your boyfriend? Lover? What?"

I turned to face him again, my body shaking in rage. "His name is William, and yes, he's my boyfriend. What is it to you? Why do you care?"

"I just came here to talk to you, Serenity. Can't I come and talk to my sister? I tried calling you, but you never answered."

"I don't answer numbers I don't recognize."

His shoulders slumped. "I've just been having a hard time. I just wanted to see if you could lend your little brother some money."

This lit a fire under my ass. "Money? You have the fucking balls to come here and ask me for money?" I freed myself of William's comforting embrace and approached my brother until we were nearly toe-to-toe. "How dare you show up here after everything you did to me. I bailed you out of jail, and you skipped town. You promised me you'd go to court, accept the plea bargain, and I'd get my money back. You almost left me homeless because I had to scramble to pay my rent. Now you are back demanding more. What nerve!"

My body tensed. I couldn't look at him. I couldn't look at the leech who would continue to suck every last penny out of me.

"Come on, Serenity. I just need a little bit to get on my feet. Things will be different this time. I got a job. It's not much, and the pay is under the table, but it pays. And my lawyer thinks the judge will go easy on me. Come on. Don't leave me hanging."

William stepped in front of me. "You heard her; she said no. So why don't you just leave." Even I could see it wasn't a question.

Dayton was speechless. Sophia was standing on the front steps behind us with her mouth agape. I was just as dumbstruck as I was over the whole situation.

"Excuse me," Dayton said, inching up to William. "But this has nothing to do with you."

"You make it my business when you don't take no as an answer and continue to harass my girlfriend. Sister or not, I won't stand by and let you continue to use her."

Even in a calm, calculated manner, William was taking charge.

"It's okay. I'll handle it," I protested.

"See?" Dayton said sarcastically to William. "Even she wants you to butt out."

William ignored me, instead walking closer to Dayton. "Like I said, why don't you leave?"

Before I could even say anything to mediate the situation, Dayton ran up to William and shoved him. William took a step back, holding his hands up as Dayton proceeded to push him again. William shoved him back defensively and headed toward his car.

I turned to Sophia. "If he doesn't leave, call the police." I hurried and got into the passenger seat. William sped off.

When we got a few blocks away from my house, he slowed down. "I'm sorry."

"For?"

"Butting into your business. And for shoving him."

"It was self-defense." I placed my hand on his right thigh. "Thanks for sticking up for me even if it was against my brother."

He sighed. "I understand how you feel now."

"What do you mean?"

He turned a corner and into a nearby parking lot and shifted into park, then turned and stared at me. "You always say you don't want to come across as using me. But after that interaction with your brother, I understand where you're coming from. I just felt angry for you. I want to be able to do nice things for you without you feeling guilty. It's just not how I imagined things, you know?"

I laid my head on his shoulder. "I wish things were different with him. I thought this last time our relationship would improve, but Dayton will never change. I accepted that I couldn't change him, and he won't change until he is ready to let go of the past and look forward to the future. I just don't want that in my life." I paused and turned so that I made eye contact with him. "I just want to focus my energy on getting back on my feet and seeing where our relationship goes."

He leaned in and kissed me. "I'd like that too. And if you'd let me, I'd love to help you put your past behind you so we can move forward into our relationship."

"How?"

"In any way I can or you feel comfortable exploring. If you want to contact old foster parents, then I'll be there for you every step of the way. If you ever choose to locate your biological father, I'll be there for you as well. No matter how small, I want to take the journey with you. I love you. I know you may not be ready to say it back, but I'm not going to keep how I feel a secret anymore."

"Thanks." I felt warm and tingly. "Thank you for being there for me. You'll never know how much I appreciate it."

"I want to help. Serenity, please let me in."

"Okay." I rubbed the nape of my neck and smiled. "I just need to figure out what it is I want. The idea of meeting my father has crossed my mind before, but it's never been a mission of mine. My brother and sister never met their fathers either. So it wasn't like I was the only one, you know? But it would be interesting to have a picture of him at least. Just to know what he looked like or even his name. Just anything." I floundered. "The past holds so many memories. Many are painful, but many made me who I want to be. Maybe someday I'll go back to that time and reclaim it. When I make a decision, I'll take you up on your offer. Deal?"

William reached over and kissed me again. "Deal! Now, how about that movie?"

I suddenly no longer had a movie on the mind. "How about a trip to the grocery store? I have something in mind." I grinned, recalling my plan to make him a homemade meal. Zina had texted me the instructions to her favourite recipe for dinner rolls, and I could make a mean stew.

William raised an eyebrow. "Oh? What ya have in mind?"

"I'm going to cook for you."

He smiled. "I won't say no to that. What do you need? I'll pay for —"

"It's on me." I reached over and kissed him. "I've set aside some money to do something nice for you. And I won't take no for an answer."

Warmth radiated throughout my entire body. After the shitty start of the day dealing with Dayton, I was looking forward to doing something for William.

"Okay! So let's go," he said excitedly.

While I didn't have tons of money, over the years I learned to stretch a dollar.

He drove to the nearest grocery store to his home. Once inside, William followed me up and down the aisles as I threw ingredients into the cart. In my head, I made a mental note of the total. I didn't want to spend all my money, and plus I had to leave room for taxes and any possible miscalculations. I didn't want William to pick up the tab, not this time at least. I reached the final aisle and threw a tin can of kidney beans into the cart. "That is everything," I told an eager William.

He grinned. "I'm pumped."

We waited in line. Of course, there was only one till was open on the busiest shopping day of the week. There were ten people in front of me, and at least half of them had nearly full carts. I sighed to myself as we waited. William bounced from foot to foot. It was cute that he was excited and impatient over something as simple as buying groceries. And this was coming from the most patient man I knew.

"Will you let me buy a bottle of wine for the occasion at least?" he asked.

I frowned on the inside because I didn't even think to budget anything to drink.

"Team effort, ya know?" he encouraged. "Or I have some leftover cider..."

I wasn't a fan of cider, but I didn't say so. "It's up to you."

"It's the least I can do as you're going to make us something so delicious. You don't even know the last time I had someone cook for me. I either eat out or heated premade meals."

That certainly added a sense of pressure. I needed to make sure I turned out something delicious that was up to his obviously high expectations. He was too nice to tell me if I sucked.

I swore to myself. Ten minutes ago, I was so excited, but now the self-doubt came barging in. I needed to keep telling myself that tonight was going to go well. And if everything went according to plan, I'd be spending the night. Slowly, one by one, the cashier rang through each customer until it came to my turn. As soon as he could reach the conveyor belt, William was already placing the items on it. I reached into my pocket for my money before he had a chance to pull a fast one.

"Thirty-five dollars and fifty cents," the cashier said after ringing through the last item.

I handed her two twenties, and she handed me my change. William helped me bag the food before leaving the store. He put the grocery bags in the back seat. "I'll be right back," he said as he made his way to the front seat.

I nodded as I got into the car. He grabbed his wallet from the center console before leaving toward the convenience store adjacent to the grocery store. *So he hadn't even taken his wallet inside the store.* My heart dropped as I imagined if I hadn't had enough money.

Soon he returned with a bottle of red wine. "I hope this is sufficient."

"It's perfect," I said with a smile.

He drove back to his place in record time. He insisted on carrying the bags in and setting them on the counter.

"Can I do anything to help?" he asked.

"No, just sit and relax."

I wasted no time as I pulled out all my ingredients. I glanced at the time on the stove. It was two in the afternoon. First thing first was preparing the dough for the dinner rolls. I mixed all the dry ingredients together then added water. I kneaded the dough a little too roughly just to get out any lingering anger suppressed inside of me. I was going to make tonight special because I intended to end this night with a bang.

William hovered over me. "I just want to see what you're doing."

"Kneading dough. Then you have to let it rise."

"Oh?"

"Then I'll start on the main course."

"I look forward to it," he whispered in my ear.

A chill rang down my back. Was he hinting at something more? Or was it all in my head?

I placed the dough in a bowl and covered it with a cloth. Then I opened up the bag of meat chunks and added a little salt and pepper, setting them aside when I was satisfied. "Do you have a large pot?" I asked, hoping and praying he did.

"Yeah, in the back of the cupboard." He dug into the back until he pulled out a large, shiny pot. It looked like it had never been used before. "Will this do?"

"Yes."

I prepared the vegetables and the seasoned meat before adding the broth then turned the heat on low and closed the lid.

"Now we wait," I said and walked over to the sofa.

"Who taught you to cook?" he asked. "I knew you could bake, but now I know you are the great cook. I mean I haven't tried it yet, but I already know it's going to be amazing."

"My mom. She is a lot of things, but she could cook."

William nodded. "My parents only knew how to cook out of a can."

"Well, you can count on me to make you a real meal."

He brushed his hand along the side of my face. "So does that mean you'll spend more time at my place? I mean… you're welcome here all the time."

"I do spend a lot of time here, so yeah."

He reached into his pocket and pulled out a key. "I want you to be able to come here whenever you want. Doesn't matter if I'm here or not. I know from what you told me that sometimes it gets stressful at your place. And I just want you to have the option of coming to my place if you need an escape."

I took the key slowly from his hand, my grasp trembling as I did so.

"The option is there."

I attached it to my own house key. "I might take you up on that offer."

"Good."

I periodically got up to check on the stew. It was coming together and it smelled so good. My dough had risen and was ready to be formed into dinner rolls. They would be the perfect companion to a perfect stew.

I put the six small rolls into a pre-greased pan and into the oven.

"Almost done, love."

He rubbed is hands together. "It smells so good."

Forty-five minutes passed until dinner was ready. The beef stew was thick and savory, and the dinner rolls were a scrumptious golden-brown, fluffy and ready for dipping. I prepared William a bowl and brought it to him.

He wasted no time taking a bite, steaming and all. "Man, it tastes better then it smells. Thanks." He took another mouthful while I waited for my bowl to cool down. I blew on it and by the time I took my first bite he was in the kitchen helping himself to a second serving.

All I could do was laugh. One thing for sure was that I could feed a healthy man. I knew it was a great recipe to a great relationship.

Before he sat down again, he cracked open the bottle of wine and brought me a glass.

"A toast to our future," he said, holding up his glass.

"I can toast to that." I beamed at him.

Then we kissed.

Tonight I was going to stay and wasn't going to take no as an answer.

Chapter 11

I moved closer to William and wrapped my arms around him as he slept. Ever since we took the plunge and I stayed the night that first time, I had been staying over two or three nights a week, and last night was no exception. I gently kissed his neck.

I took a few large breaths and savored the moment as I longed for the hunk lying beside me. "Good morning," I whispered in his ear.

William turned to me and we shared a look of love. Then his lips parted, and a silly grin crossed his face. "Good morning!"

It was late Sunday morning and neither of us had to go to work, but I didn't want to sleep in any longer. I wanted to get up and do something. William reached over and kissed me.

"What do you want to do today?" he asked.

It was as if he read my mind. "Grab breakfast?" I suggested.

"Or we could stay in bed." His cheeks glowed as he smiled at me. "Whatever your heart desires."

I chuckled. "How about we get donuts?"

"Is that a joke about how much I love sweets? Cause you're right."

I threw my hands up and sighed exasperatedly. "You're right. You got me."

We both laughed.

I reached over and kissed him once more. "I'm gonna use the bathroom and get dressed. We can go from there, all right?"

He pulled the comforter off the both of us. "All right."

"Hey!" I attempted to snatch the comforter back, but William gently resisted my attempts.

He raised an eyebrow at me. "I thought you were ready to get up."

I smirked. "Yeah!"

"I'm helping you out, hun."

I shook my head and hit his arm playfully. I grabbed my phone off the end table and strolled into the bathroom. Even though it was William's apartment, my belongings had found their way into all sorts of random nooks and crannies. A toothbrush in the bathroom, my hair spray on the counter, even special milk in his fridge.

I sat down on the edge of the tub and checked my messages.

What are you up to? Mom had texted me.

Shortly after talking with Zina, I had realized I missed my mom. I accepted that I couldn't always rely on her, but after Dayton stopped by, I just wanted any connection with my family that I could get, even if it was only crumbs being thrown my way. So I messaged my mom and told her I forgave her. I knew that I only had two choices if I wanted to maintain any kind of relationship with her: I could keep fighting a losing battle, or I could let go of thoughts of the outcome and enjoy what time I could get with her.

I'm good, I replied.

I heard from Dayton the other day, Mom replied a minute

later.

Oh? How did that go? After I sent the message, my heart sped up. I hadn't spoken to Dayton since the altercation in front of my house. I wondered if he was back in jail.

He wanted some money. So I sent him a little bit. He told me he wants to change his life around. He also told me your boyfriend assaulted him.

I gritted my teeth.

Did Dayton mention that he harassed me for money???? I sent the message quickly before immediately typing a follow-up. *And that after I said no, he kept on and on until William had to step in to tell him to back off and Dayton pushed him. So don't believe his sob story.*

My hands trembled. How dare he blame William.

There was a knock on the door. "Serenity?"

"I'm almost done."

"No rush, hun. I was just going to run to the store quickly for some milk. You want anything?"

"I'm good, thanks."

The green light on my phone blinked, signaling another text.

I just wish you kids would get along. I won't be around forever.

If only she knew. I wanted a *relationship* with Dayton and Harmony, not a one-sided connection where I was on the giving side and they never reciprocated. How was that fair to me? How was life, in general, fair to me? A bitter taste formed in my mouth. I should be grateful for what I had, but I couldn't help but wonder what could have been.

None of us will be here forever, I texted back. *I just hope Dayton does turn a new leaf so I can have a relationship with him. But life is too short to spend time and energy on people who can't help themselves.*

I clicked out of my messages and waddled into the living room where I slumped down on the couch. Soon William would be back and we'd enjoy a hearty day together like we usually did on our days off. I reached for the remote and turned on the television. The background noise drowned out the oppressive silence. My phone vibrated and, against my better judgment, I checked it.

Serenity. Everyone makes mistakes. I know I've made plenty and I understand to some degree what Dayton is going through. Don't be hard on him. I just wish when I was in that dark place I had some support.

I could have rolled my eyes and replied bitterly, but I didn't. Her words concerned me. Mom had made many mistakes, but what did she mean when she said that she knew what Dayton was going through? As far as I knew, she wasn't a criminal. She was a terrible mother with a hard upbringing, but a criminal? No, it couldn't be. Mom's worst attribute was shacking up with questionable men in order to get by (which would explain her relationship with Mike). So what was "that dark place"?

What do you mean you know what Dayton is going through?

I threw her a bone because I wanted to know more. Mom didn't talk much about her past. All I ever really got out of her was that her parents abused her and she had to take care of herself and Aunt Jane. Aunt Jane didn't offer much more.

It's nothing, she replied.

I sighed. Of course it was nothing. It's always "nothing" with Mom. Why did I expect anything different?

Before I could dwell on the matter any longer, the door opened and William walked in. "I see you're not dressed yet," he said.

I glanced down at my tank top and pajama pants. "I guess

not."

He set a bag on the counter and frowned at me. "What's wrong?"

I sighed and handed him the phone. "Check for yourself." Maybe he'd have some kind of insight.

I waited as William read today's correspondence with my mother. He handed me back the phone.

"I know it doesn't get easier, Serenity." He pulled me into a tight embrace.

I laid my head on his shoulder. "I know, but I can't wrap my mind around her last message."

"Oh?"

A heavy sigh escaped my lips. "I'm probably overthinking it, but she said she knew where Dayton was coming from, and when I asked her about it, she shut me down. I know it means something. I just wish I knew what." My mind spun around like a racecar losing control on a track. What could Mom have gotten in trouble for? And when? Mom couldn't even stand up to men who treated her like crap, so that crossed out a whole slew of crimes. It just didn't make sense.

William straightened his posture and held me at arm's length. "Has she ever been arrested?"

I shook my head. "Not that I know of."

William pressed his hands against his temples for a moment. "You mentioned that she doesn't talk much about the past, right?" He paused, then immediately said, "I'm sorry for probing."

I perked up, ignoring his last comment. "So do you think she could have had trouble with the law? That could contribute to why we were taken from her." While the probability seemed unlikely, the more I thought about it, the

LEAVING THE PIECES BEHIND

more sense it made. It quickly dawned on me that I didn't really know my mother as well as I thought I did.

"Could be?" William said tentatively.

I pressed my lips tight. "But how do I find out?" The question wasn't directed at William.

"An internet search may be a good place to start."

"Oh, good idea!"

William rose without a word and headed for the bedroom. He returned with his laptop and handed it to me. My fingertips paused over the keyboard, wondering what to type first.

"Maybe try her full name and the city and state where she lives," William suggested softly.

I could have smacked my head. *Duh*. I knew how to look people up on the internet. It wasn't that long ago that I had searched for my brother.

I typed my mother's name, Melody Grace Rupert, and the city she lived in into the search bar. I scrolled through the results, searching for a news article or something, but came up empty. I sighed.

William stroked my shaking hand. "I can help you out if you want."

"I appreciate it. I just want to know what she's hiding. She's always hiding something from me."

William took the laptop from me. I hovered over him, resting my head on his shoulder. If anyone would know what to do, it'd be him. *If* there was anything to find, that is.

William pulled up a state database from the area where Mom lived. "We're in luck! Her state has an online database with a list of criminal cases going back forty years."

He typed in my mother's name. *No record.*

"Did she go by an alias?" he asked.

I gave him a funny look. "A what?"

"Like another name. Was she ever married?"

I shook my head. "No, Rupert is her maiden name."

He took a deep breath. "How long has she lived there?"

I shrugged. "A few years. Before that, she lived in our home state."

"Okay, that gives us something to work with."

He closed out of that tab, opened another, and went to the database for where my mom used to live. A few minutes into the search, he sighed.

"What?" I asked.

"This will be harder than it looks."

"Can't you just search her name?"

"Unfortunately, no."

I glanced away and sighed. *Great. Another roadblock. What is Mom hiding? Or not hiding?* I didn't even know what I was looking for or if there was anything to find. The town I was born in was so close to where I lived now, but I never visited. It seemed like everyone was keeping secrets, and Mom always said that leaving that town was the best decision she ever made. I hadn't any real reason to return to the town. I had no friends, and I had no recollection of any family I may have had there anyway.

"Don't look so gloomy, hun. I never said I couldn't search. Just that it might be difficult."

I leaned over and hugged him. "Hmm. Maybe later. Let's go eat." I didn't want to dwell on this because I knew that it would only serve to put me in a bad mood, and I didn't want to ruin my day off with William.

"Go get dressed, then we'll go."

I shrugged. "Or I can go like this." I didn't want to get

dressed. Pajama pants were so comfy.

"All right." He smiled. "It's just you normally don't go out in public like that."

I smiled. "Well, today is different."

He laughed. "I guess so."

We wasted no time jumping in his car. I was glad to be getting out of the house. My stomach rumbled loudly.

"I know how you feel," William chuckled. "I want a big, hearty breakfast with bacon, ham, eggs, hash browns, and toast."

"So, in other words, you want to eat the entire menu?"

William glanced at me and smiled widely. "I'm a hungry guy."

"And a hungry guy needs to be well-fed."

"You do a good job of that."

William always said I made good meals. The past few weeks, random ingredients that I had never seen in his fridge suddenly appeared, like asparagus and avocado. He loved when I made pesto chicken, or homemade guacamole and kale chips, or even something as simple as steamed asparagus. I blessed William's heart. He was a hard worker, charming, and would help anyone in need, but he couldn't cook. If something didn't come from a can or couldn't be nuked in the microwave, he wouldn't make it.

All the thought of food made me hungry, so I was glad when we arrived at the diner. It seemed as if most of our dates ended up at a hole-in-the-wall place or another similar eatery. I secretly wanted more variety, but I guessed monotony happened when couples became comfortable. It was nice to let my guard down and not overthink everything, yet I still did. My mother's mysterious words plagued me.

William ordered himself the Big Monster Breakfast: three sausages, three pieces of bacon, a hamsteak, three eggs, two pieces of toast, and homemade hash browns. I didn't know where he'd put it all. I settled on two fluffy pancakes.

William and I made small talk — mostly about food — but I struggled to concentrate on what he was saying because I couldn't help but think about Mom. It was so typical of me. Maybe deep down I didn't accept Mom for who she was. Maybe I wanted more, some kind of truth. I knew I was sick of the secrets.

"You're still thinking about it, aren't you?" William asked, shoving a giant slice of ham in his mouth and chewing thoughtfully.

I nodded, pushing around the last few bites of pancake on my plate. "I just can't help it. Sorry."

He fiddled with his fork and stopped eating. "Didn't you say your hometown was around here?"

I smiled slightly. He was reading my mind again. "Yeah, about fifty miles north of here. Why?" I told him the town name as he looked something up on his phone.

He took a sip of his water. "This may be a long shot, but how would you like to take a road trip after breakfast? It says here that their local library is open until four."

"Oh?" I smiled at him, but I was still confused. "Why do we need their library when there's a perfectly good one downtown?"

"Well, I was thinking maybe we could check out their archives. I'm no detective, but maybe we can find an article or something about your past. I mean, just because you don't think she was arrested for anything doesn't mean it didn't happen before you were born or maybe when you least expected it."

My eyes lit up. "Why didn't I think of that?"

William beamed at me.

I shifted in my seat. While my small hometown only had a population of about five thousand, there would still be a ton of content to skim through because the records probably covered the neighboring villages and towns. I blew a series of short breaths, anything really to calm my nerves. I wasn't sure what I was hoping to find. I always wondered about where Mom came from and why she was always so apprehensive to tell us.

She always tried her best for us kids, but always seemed to come up short. As I got older and tried to ask her questions about her past, she would close up and not say a thing. Why? Could the answer be why she didn't want me to find my father?

I remember one time I asked Mom about my dad. She had been sitting on the couch, reading a cookbook, and she was in one of her moods. It was Father's Day and I was one of the only ones in my class without a father. I had made a card and hid it under my pillow, but I wanted a dad to give it to, so I had asked her, "Where's my dad?"

Mom had looked up from her book, brushing her hair from her face. There were dark circles under her eyes, and her eyebrows furrowed. She frowned and told me, "He was no good." She had called him *a sperm donor,* but I knew she didn't mean it literally. I knew there was a story there. When I had tried to push further, she had sent me to my room. I remember thinking that she really didn't like my father, but why? I never could get a straight answer out of her.

I continued to pick at my plate while William scarfed down the last of his meal as if he hadn't eaten in a week. I wasn't hungry anymore. My appetite wasn't there. I bounced my leg. I really was hoping, praying, and looking forward to getting some answers. I knew it was going to be a wild goose chase, but I was still hoping to catch a break, even a tiny one. I'd been let down so many times that I was immune to the depressing notion that this may be another dead end.

"Hurry and eat," William urged, breaking me out of my stupor.

I stared down at my unfinished plate. I forced one more bite. I was grateful William cared. He was spending his day and wasting his gas to help me.

After a few more bites, I made eye contact with William who had already finished his breakfast. "Where do you put all that food?" I asked lightheartedly.

He patted his stomach. "In here. It builds strength."

"You and your high metabolism," I replied with a chuckle. "If I ate all that, it'd go straight for my hips." I wasn't big by any means, but any weight I did accumulate went right for the butt region, making me rather "pear shaped" as my mother had once called me. William seemed to like it.

"Are you ready to go?" he asked, pulling out his wallet and slapping two bills on the table.

I jumped up a little too quickly. "Yes."

"Anything else before we hit the road?" he asked once we were in the car.

I thought about my pajama pants and how ridiculous I probably looked, but I shook my head. I just wanted to get there and get answers.

The ride on the highway dragged by. William talked about random things I found myself nodding along to. I barely listened as my mind was occupied and guilt consumed me. I couldn't help it.

"We're almost there," he announced when we passed a sign stating the town was only a few miles ahead.

I looked at my phone for the address of the library. "Cain Street. The library is on Cain Street."

"I know, I already punched it into my GPS."

I lowered my head. Of course, he was prepared. It was his idea to come here in the first place.

We reached the town, and he dropped his speed to twenty. We passed the little ice cream shop that was now boarded up. "Mr. Holt used to sell the best ice cream," I told William as I pointed out the window at the derelict building.

We continued through downtown which was mostly empty businesses. We passed a small store which had antiques on display, and a couple of little bistros with cute sandwich boards on the sidewalk. I didn't recognize any of them, and the store fronts I did recognize were blurry remnants in the back of my brain. I sighed. "I remember when we moved out of here when I was five. It was a sad day."

While I was still young, I had so many fond memories of the place. My early days were some of my simplest. It was after we moved that Mom became more depressed. She started dating a man name Gino for a few months, and then another man named Tony or something. She changed after that. None of her boyfriends stood out much; I didn't even really remember what they looked like. The only one I really remembered was Mike, and as an adult I now realized that he was a pig. I'd never know what Mom saw in him. I always wondered why Mom didn't stay with any of our biological fathers. Like me, Harmony and Dayton didn't have contact with their dads.

William pulled up in front of a brick building with a

fading sign that may have read, *Library.* "We're here."

I reached over, pecked him on the cheek, and exited the vehicle.

A woman in an oversized red dress greeted us when we entered the library. "Can I help you?" She beamed at us.

"We're looking for your news archive," William said.

She nodded quickly and happily like a bobble head doll. "Is there any particular year you're looking for?"

I looked at William who never broke eye contact with the librarian.

"Can we start with the years 1990 to 1994?"

She nodded. I felt embarrassed. It should have been me doing the talking.

She led us to a back room filled with old microfilm readers. "Let me know if you need anything."

"Thanks, we will," William replied.

Once she was out of sight, he closed the door to the small room. "I'll start with articles from 1990 and you start with 1991, okay? If we split it up, we can get through them quicker."

"Okay," I agreed.

I sat and scrolled through the archives, scanning the headlines for anything linking to my mother. There was one about a bar fight resulting in a man and a woman being arrested on January 3, 1991. Mom was only seventeen in 1991, so not old enough to go to the bar. I kept scrolling through the headlines when I stopped suddenly at something that I thought held some relevance. It was an article about a missing teenager: "March 5, 1991, 15-year-old Jane Rupert was last seen leaving her residence at 11pm on March 3rd." I skimmed the rest of the article, looking for any mention of a Melody Rupert. There was no mention of my mother, but it was something.

"William."

He turned to look at me. "Did you find something?"

"No mention of my mother, but I found a report of my aunt going missing in early 1991. It probably doesn't mean anything, but at least I can confirm that my mom was in this town around this time. I'm not surprised that my aunt went missing. She likely was a runaway."

Mom always promised to give us a better life than she had growing up. She never had to grow up in foster care, but she came from a life of addiction and abuse. She was eighteen or nineteen when she moved out of her parents' house.

"Keep looking," William said. "I have a feeling we're onto something."

I smiled. "Thanks for helping me."

He stopped and touched my thigh. "I promised to help you come to terms with your past. And if finding answers are what you need, then I'll be here."

I reached over and kissed him. "Thanks."

He grinned before getting back to the task at hand.

I continued flipping through articles going into April and May. Nothing more about my aunt missing. I know she eventually was found, but the fact that she was never mentioned again was concerning to me.

I had scrolled until the end of the year but found nothing. I sighed. "Nothing. Have you had any better luck?"

William shook his head. "No. 1990 was a boring year."

"Same with 1991."

"But I'm going to go ahead with 1992," he said.

"I'll take '93 then." William and I made a great team, and I don't know if I would have even thought of doing this in the first place, never mind skimming through hundreds of old records.

I skimmed through nearly all of 1993 when the librarian opened the door.

"How is everything going in here?" she asked.

"Good," William said.

"I'm just letting you know the library is closing in fifteen minutes."

I sighed. I knew that this was time-consuming, but I had thought we had more time.

"Okay, thanks," I said, eager to get back to the search.

"Is there anything I can help you with?"

"No, thanks," William replied. As she went to leave, he stood. "Actually, there is something you may be able to help with."

She stopped and smiled. "Oh?"

"I don't know if you've lived in this town long, but we're looking to find any information on a woman who used to live here. Maybe you know her."

The librarian leaned against the door. "I moved in the early nineties and just moved back last year, but I might be able to help."

I stood, staring at this woman. Could she know my mother?

"Melody Rupert," I said.

The librarian turned to me and bit her lip. "I haven't heard that name in a long time."

"Please, anything you can tell me about her, I'd appreciate."

The librarian took a step back. "Why do you want to know? How do you know Melody?"

"She's my mother." I took a deep breath. "I'm Serenity,

her daughter. So, please, you need to tell me." I knew I sounded desperate, but who wouldn't be if they had a huge question mark following them around? Or had a mother who was great at hiding things? This woman here could be the missing link to explain why my mom was the way she was.

"Serenity Rupert. Oh my darn. I remember you. You were only a few months when I last spoke with Melody. What can I tell you?"

I paused for a moment. "Anything."

"Melody and I used to hang out in the neighborhood back in the '80s. She never wanted to leave my house. Said my mother made the best meals. But I doubt that is what you want to know."

"Did you know my father? Was my mother dating anyone?" I asked eagerly.

The librarian stopped for a moment. "No, not that recalled. She was shy and didn't go out much. But she did have a crush on this one man. He was a few years older than her; a high school drop-out. Now to think of his name. Samuel. And I think his last name was Anderson or something."

"Robertson?" William offered. "I remember coming across a Samuel Robertson while I was looking through the archives," he explained.

The librarian smiled. "Yes, Robertson. Samuel Robertson." She glanced at her wristwatch. "I really must get ready to close up. I hope I helped in any way."

"Thank you so much," I said. "We'll be sure to clean up on our way out."

Inside the car, I rocked back and forth. "Samuel Robertson," I repeated quietly to myself. So many thoughts were going through my mind. Could he be my father? Or maybe he knew my father. "I need to find him."

William patted my shoulder. "I know you're anxious, but maybe it's best to stop a minute and think this over."

"What do you mean?"

"I came across that name a few times while I was looking through the archives. In much of the '90s, a Samuel Robertson was arrested several times for bar fights and disturbing the peace. So if this is the same person, it's evident there is some dysfunction."

I took a deep breath. "Then what should I do?"

"Maybe text your mom, ask her about that man. Even if you have to stretch the truth a bit."

"Stretch the truth how?"

"Maybe say a man by the name of Samuel Robertson messaged you and said he knew her. Her reaction may tell you a lot."

I nodded. "Good idea. You know, you are so full of ideas today."

He kissed me on the forehead. "I just want you to find the truth."

I pulled out my phone, took a deep breath, and whispered, "Here goes nothing."

Do you know a Samuel Robertson? He says he knows you, I texted her.

How she responded could be the answer to the almost twenty-four-year mystery of who my biological father was.

Chapter 12

I didn't want to call my mom until I was back at William's apartment. In the meantime, she had sent me a flurry of texts, all begging me to call her. I glanced over at William who was focused on the road probably in his own little world. Like me, he internalized things rather than talked about them. We were more alike than either of us wished to admit.

He caught my glance. "What are you thinking about?" he asked.

"I'm just trying to think about what my mom is going to say. It's obvious the name hit a nerve. She keeps texting me."

"Why not call her?"

I shrugged. "I don't feel like doing it in the car. I don't know. I might get emotional."

"Okay?" He moved his right hand from the steering wheel to my left thigh. "I don't mind, Serenity. I can only imagine the thoughts going through your mind."

Samuel Robertson was on my mind. All I had was a name and a huge question mark following it. Who was he? Was he my biological father or just my mother's fling, one of her many lovers over the years? I stared at the last text message from Mom, and the chances of him being just another man with no meaning seemed unlikely.

Please call me, Serenity. Don't talk to him anymore until you call me.

What are you hiding Mom? I thought. *What is it about Samuel Robertson that makes you so afraid?* But the only way I'd find out was by asking her. I needed to keep my story straight and not lead her on to my suspicions.

I sighed, resolving myself to just get it over with. "I'll do it. I'm going to call her. Wish me well, William."

He flashed me a smile. "You'll do fine, Hun."

I dialed her number. The phone rang several times before my mom picked up.

"Serenity!" There was a pause and heavy breathing on the other end. "Okay, I'm glad you called. Um..."

"Take a deep breath." I gnawed at my upper lip, trying to keep my rising anxiety at bay. I heard Mom exhale a laboured breath. "Okay, better?"

"Yes. What did he say? Tell me exactly what Samuel said."

Dots of perspiration formed on my forehead as I swallowed several times. "He asked me if I knew you."

"Okay, and?"

"I told him I did, and then I asked him how he knew you."

My mom's voice became a little more frantic, but she maintained her calm. "And what did he say? And what did you say back? Don't leave anything out, please."

I fiddled with the collar of my shirt. "He said he knew you from back in the day and just wanted to reconnect."

I glanced at William who mouthed, "Ask her who he is."

"She doesn't know," she whispered back, covering the speaker of my phone.

"Who is he, Mom?" I blurted. "And don't tell me no one." Mom wasn't going to hide this from me, I wouldn't let her. She wasn't going to drag this out a moment longer. Either she told me who he was, or I would hunt him down and ask him myself. My posture stiffened.

"He's no one," she said.

"Okay, fine, don't tell me. I'm going to ask him myself how he knows you."

"No, you can't. Don't!" The desperation in her voice was chilling.

"Mom, you either tell me who he is, or I'll message him back and ask him, which I think I'll end up doing anyway, but I'll give you the chance first."

There was a silence.

"Okay, Mom. It's fine. I'm going to message him myself. I'm not playing games with you." Without waiting for a response, I hung up.

William stared at me.

"She'll call back," I told him. I knew Mom.

And less than two minutes later she called me back and I answered. "Hello?"

"Please, Serenity, don't ask him. Don't message him. Forget he exists."

"What are you hiding from me? Why don't you want me to know who he is? What is the big secret? Because if you don't tell me, I'll find out. I'm so sick of you lying."

She took a deep breath. She mumbled something under her breath. "He's… well… he's your *sperm donor*." She said the last word with such malice that it took me off guard for a moment, but I quickly recovered.

She had finally admitted it. Samuel Robertson was my father, or according to Mom, my "sperm donor." So what was so bad about him? Why did she want to keep him away from me?

Before I could inquire further, she continued, her voice on edge. "There. Are you happy? Now leave it alone, Serenity. You don't want to know him. You are better off without him. Block him." I could hear her voice crack. "Just leave it be. Some things are better left in the past, and he is one of them."

"Why?" I asked. I wasn't going to give up so easily. "How bad can he be? He seemed like a successful person based on his profile," I lied.

"It's all lies. Don't believe anything he says," Mom continued before her voice became slightly quieter. "He isn't who you think he is. We went out for a few weeks, and then he broke my heart. He left me, Serenity. He was into drugs, and last I heard he was in and out of jail. He wasn't a good guy. He pretends to be, but he isn't. Please, just let it go."

My chest ached. So she kept me from my father because he left her. The librarian had said that they never went out, that Mom only had a little crush. Was the librarian confusing a relationship with some casual sex? Did my mom actually love him? Did he even want me? My mom never had a great track record with men, and she always got her heart broken.

The world around me slowed to a standstill.

"Did you hear me?" My mom's voice was becoming firmer, almost angry.

I took a deep breath. "Yes, I heard you, Mom. I heard you loud and clear."

"So will you please let this go?" Her voice became gentle once more.

"How bad can he really be, Mom?" I asked, more rhetorically than anything else. How bad *could* he be? "I mean, how much worse could it get? Considering I spent half my life with strangers anyway. Some better than others. I have to know, Mom. I have to know if he wanted me. Why wasn't he there for me? For us? Why didn't he love me?"

I heard some soft crying on the other end.

"Don't cry, Mom. It's not your fault."

She mumbled a weak, "Yes, it is."

"I just want to know who he is. That other part of me, you know? He may be the worst person in the world, and you could have my best interests in heart when you made the choice you did, but I deserve to know. I deserve to know what kind of person he is. It has nothing to do with you now."

"I never wanted you to get hurt, Serenity. I'm sorry for everything. I'm sorry that I keep letting you down. You, Dayton, and Harmony, I keep letting you all down."

"Then please do this one thing for me, Mom. If you know where he lives or anything more about him, you have to tell me. I just need closure. I don't expect a relationship with him. But I need to know. Please."

She wasn't going to tell me, I knew it. But I had to try. Mom was the link to the truth. She was the link to the other half of my history that I had no part of. I had convinced myself long ago that it was all right that I didn't know him. I thought I had accepted that I'd never know him, but here I was, trying to get the truth out of my mom.

"His sister — your aunt, I guess you can call her — lives not too far from you; her name is Claire Marrows. I've kept my eye on her over the years. Last I checked a few months ago, she still lived there and worked at *Perry's Market*. As for where your... father..." She choked the word out. "...is, I don't know."

"Thanks, Mom."

There was a pause. "He never messaged you, did he?"

I sighed. "No, he didn't. I was sleuthing for answers and

came across the name."

She took a deep breath. "Should have known that son-of-a-bitch never would've messaged you."

I looked out the window at the city limits. "I'll talk to you later, Mom."

"Just don't say I never warned you, Serenity." Her voice was suddenly clipped, a complete one-eighty from before, then *click*. She hung up on me like I knew she would.

I quickly searched for *Perry's Market* on my phone to see if it was still open for the day. It was.

"Do you think we can make a pit stop?" I asked William.

"For sure. Where to?"

"*Perry's Market*. If my mom's telling the truth, my father's sister, Claire Marrows, works there."

"Okay, but I want to come inside with you. You don't know any of these people."

I nodded and returned to my thoughts.

Maybe William was a little over-protective, but I appreciated it all the same. I couldn't help but wonder, though, what could possibly happen inside a building full of people? This Claire Marrows may not be there or even work there anymore. Maybe she wasn't there at all and Mom was sending me off on a wild goose chase. All the possibilities were going to drive me crazy, but this Claire Marrows was my only hope to finding my biological father, and I had a list of questions I wanted answered. Like where he had been for the last twenty-four years. Or what happened that made Mom hate him enough that she'd keep him from me.

"We are just pulling up now," William said, pulling me out of my stupor.

We reached a small brick building. We were the only ones in the parking lot. The sign outside told us that *Perry's Market* was a local grocer, not the typical supermarket. From the car, I could see a woman in her early twenties stocking a shelf. Surely she wasn't Claire. We walked inside and right by her toward the front till.

"Can I help you?" the woman behind the till asked. Her long curly hair — same texture as mine — covered her name tag.

"Um, yeah," I paused, biting my lip. Could I do this? I stuck out my chin, my resolve firm. "I'm looking for Claire Marrows."

The woman's eyes narrowed. "Do I know you?"

William rubbed my back. "Um, no," I said. My throat itched. What if Mom was lying again, or what if she didn't want to tell me anything about my father? I gnawed at my nails as I wondered if coming here at all was a good idea.

"Okay… so what can I do for you?" She had one hand on the counter and one by her side out of sight. She peered at me, curious but almost bored.

I gulped. At least she wasn't angry or demanding, unlike Mom. "Have you heard of my mother?" I paused to catch a breath. *Damnit!* I was going to fuck this up before I even got the words out of my mouth. "She was involved with your brother Samuel Robertson, and she said you'd know where to find him." Once I'd said it, sweat beaded on my forehead as my brain started swirling in multiple directions.

She twisted her upper lip. "I don't know who you are, or why you want to talk to Samuel, but you better have a good reason."

From the corner of my eye, I saw the employee we saw earlier scurry toward the back.

William cleared his throat. "Look, I'm sorry we showed

up here unannounced. My girlfriend's mother, Melody Rupert, told her that Samuel is her biological father."

Claire gasped, her angry look dissipating and her hand flying to cover her mouth.

"I know this is sudden," I tried to explain. "I just found out myself, but I need to know where to find Samuel. I have so many questions, I mean… Please, do you know where he is?"

Claire took a step back. "I remember her. Melody." She swore something under her breath.

What had my mom done?

"She told me you'd know where to find him," I pressed. "I don't want any money or anything like that from him. I just need to know. Please."

I swore I could almost see a hint of pity in her eyes, but I didn't care. I just needed answers.

Claire shook her head. "I doubt he'd want anything to do with that woman. Whether or not she's your mama, she is no good. And I don't think he had a child with her."

My heart fell and I tried in vain to push the tears back from my eyes.

She sighed. "Give me your number and I'll pass it on. But don't count on it."

A little bit of hope blossomed when she said that. With a heavy sigh and realizing I had no other choice, I agreed. She passed me a slip of paper and I wrote down my first and last name — in case he didn't remember my mother — and under it my cell number. I just hope he'd contact me. Claire took the piece of paper from me and studied it.

"Serenity…" She stared at me intensely. "I'll make sure to let him know. Now you and your *friend* here either buy something or make your exit."

I gave a weak *thank you* and we left the market.

"She was not a very pleasant woman," I said once we got back into the car.

William glanced away for a moment. "No, she wasn't."

"What's wrong?"

He scrubbed the back of his neck. "Probably nothing, but something about her rubbed me the wrong way."

I nodded. "I know what you mean." She was rude, but something about her denial, her defensiveness, made me suspicious.

We sat for a few minutes in silence before pulling away from the curb. For a half-mile or so, William lightly tapped the steering wheel, his lips pursed.

"What are you thinking about?" I asked tenderly.

He continued to stare at the road ahead of him. "I have a friend who I'm going to ask to look into both Claire Marrows' and Samuel Robertson's backgrounds."

"Oh? Why?" My heart skipped a beat. What did he have on his mind?

"I care about you, and I don't want to see you get hurt. It could be that Claire is suspicious, but I just want to rule out any dangers. Do you understand?"

"Yeah." I smiled. He'd read my mind, and I reveled in our connection. "I appreciate it."

When we returned to his flat and sat in his parking spot, William moved closer. His cheeks were glowing, his gaze intense. Without a sound, I leaned in, and our lips sealed. As the tension left my body, I entered a place of tranquility.

When we parted, our eyes connected, shining. I stroked his hand. He was my guardian angel and had entered my life at its lowest point. My heart sped up. I reached in again, my hand grasping the back of his neck as I pulled him closer. His wet lips caused my body to go wild, like fireworks cracking at midnight on New Year's Eve. Our lips lingered until we parted for the second time. I peered into his eyes, and a smile spread across my face, from cheek to cheek. "Thank you for helping me today." He had done so much for me; there was no way I'd be able to repay him.

He grinned, placing his hands on my shoulders. "I'd do anything for you. I'll get that background check done, and then you'll get to know your dad." He wavered for a moment, moving his hands to meet mine. "But know no matter what, I'll be here for you."

A tear formed in my eye, and I opened my mouth to speak, but no words came out. It was on the tip of my tongue, whatever it was. Just his presence brought me to my knees, made me feel safe, happy, and grateful.

William wiped away the tear. "Do you want to go pick up takeout and maybe watch a movie before going to bed?"

I nodded.

Half an hour had passed when we went inside his place, food in hand, and sat on the sofa. Our legs brushed. At that moment as we ate I realized how lucky I was.

"William," I said.

He swallowed his food. "Yeah?"

"I love you."

It came out of nowhere, but I meant it. I did.

He smiled, and we embraced. "I love you, too."

Chapter 13

I scrambled around William's apartment looking for something to wear. I hadn't been home in four nights, and with everything that had been going on, it never crossed my mind to do some laundry. I took a second look in the bedroom for a clean shirt. Anything. As I searched, William strolled into the dimly-lit bedroom wearing only his boxers.

"Are you looking for something?" he asked, lounging on the edge of the unmade bed.

I sighed, plopping down next to him. "Something to wear."

He gently rubbed my shoulder. "We can stop by your place so you can find something to put on, but we'd have to get going soon."

"What time is it?"

"Shortly after four."

I groaned. I didn't want to go to work. I wanted to crawl back under the covers and cuddle. William smirked, reached over, and kissed me gently on the forehead. "I have to work late tonight, but tomorrow I get off early and we could have some alone time."

I forced a smile. "I should go home and do some laundry... and my share of the housework."

William laughed.

"Can we just skip work? Pretend we're sick or

something?" I reached over and pulled the shirt I wore yesterday over my head. It was wishful thinking, but the reality was that the bills wouldn't pay themselves.

"I wish I could, Serenity. But on the bright side, my friend is supposed to get back to me today with those background checks."

That piqued my interest. I stopped and stared at William. "Oh!"

"Any calls from Samuel?"

I took a deep breath and sighed. "No, but it's only been a few days. I wonder if my mom warned him I was coming or something." I wouldn't have put it past her. She had sent me a few texts over the last couple days, asking me to reconsider. I wanted to reply to her so badly, but I knew that my response would be brutal and hurt her feelings. She never gave me a straight answer about what made Samuel so bad and why she never gave him a chance. Maybe my life would have been different if she had.

I finished getting dressed as William slipped on his dress shoes. I stared down at my bare feet. Today was going to be one of those days — the I'm-not-going-to-wear-socks kind of day. I grabbed a hair tie from the end table and quickly yanked my disheveled, uncombed hair into a messy bun.

"Are you ready to go?"

I nodded. "What time is it now?"

"Four-twenty."

I forced myself to the door. Why was my body dragging itself along? Work wasn't terrible. In fact, I enjoyed it. Maybe it was because I knew that I wouldn't be spending the night with William. I had become so accustomed to staying over at his place that having to sleep in my own bed seemed foreign to me.

I stared out the window during the short drive to my place.

"I'll wait for you," he said as we pulled up.

The lights in my house were on. Did Sophia have a party last night? I had been so busy hanging out with William that I hadn't even met our new roommate yet. Crystal had moved out a few weeks ago.

I walked inside and found Sophia passed out on the couch with an empty bottle of vodka nearby. I tiptoed around her into the hallway and was making my way toward my bedroom when the bathroom door opened. I jumped.

A woman − my new roommate − staggered out of the bathroom. "Who are you? Party is over."

I bit my lip. "Um, I live here." The pit in my stomach tightened. Who has a party on a Tuesday night?

She glared at me, and her mouth twisted as stale booze radiated off her breath.

"I have to get ready for work, so if you'd excuse me." I walked past her and stopped at my door. A few weeks ago, Crystal announced she was moving out, so I had installed a lock on my door not knowing who was going to be replacing her. Thankfully, my room didn't seem to have been disturbed in my absence. Not that I had many possessions anyway. I quickly changed into a clean t-shirt and pair of pants. I had been leaving my aprons at work and washing them as needed. Just as when I worked at *George's*, I became more relaxed at this new bakery as time passed.

I left my room, locking the door behind me, and headed toward the front door when I was stopped by my new roommate.

"Who are you? If you really live here, how come I've

never seen you until now?"

"I'm Serenity. And you are?" I asked as politely as possible as I rubbed the back of my neck. The last thing I wanted was conflict.

"Sarah."

"Well, I've really got to go. Tell Sophia I said hi and that I'll be home tonight."

She mumbled something that I didn't catch, but I didn't care.

I hurried out to the car where William was anxiously waiting.

"Sorry I took so long. I met my *new* roommate," I said when I got into the car.

"Oh? How was she?"

"I think she was drunk. So not a good first impression."

William frowned. "I'm sorry to hear that, hun."

I shrugged. "Maybe once she sobers up, I'll have a different impression. I think I might have caught her off guard. Can we just go now?"

He obliged without another word.

After a short drive, William pulled up in front of the bakery. He pulled me into a big hug like always. I smiled, and the embrace lingered. I didn't want to let go yet. But finally I forced myself to release him.

"I'll pick you up tomorrow morning, okay?" William said.

"Okay, have a good day. I love you."

"I love you too." We shared one last kiss before I headed into work. It was so freeing to say those words without constraint. William checked off every box. I was grateful for him, but I was also proud for staying true to my feelings. I made sure he was for real, before I showed him my true self.

Zina opened the door for me. "Well, good morning."

"Good morning!"

I nearly floated by her. I was glad to be at work, back where there was a sense of normalcy. After spending a few minutes in the back bathroom and tying a fresh apron around my waist, I was ready to begin my day.

"Did you spend the night with that hunk again?" Zina asked.

I grinned. "Yup. But I also stopped at my place and met the new roomie for the first time." Though it was unintentional, I let a slight bit of dismay leak into my voice.

"Don't care for her?"

I shrugged. "When your first time meeting someone is when she's drunk and acting like you don't live there, then yeah, I guess I would say that my first impression wasn't great." At the same time, I would have probably acted the same way that Sarah did, only I wouldn't tell Zina that.

Zina kneaded the dough. "I had my share of bad roommates in my day."

"I'm just waiting for the day I don't need one." I knew I'd be stuck with a roommate until I found a better paying job, got a promotion, or the best option, moved in with William.

"It'll come," she reassured me.

My hands were on autopilot preparing the day's cinnamon roll orders.

"Sooner or later," I whispered.

"So, I take it things are progressing with William." Zina peeked at me with a raised eyebrow.

"Yes." I smiled. I had been processing everything that had happened over the last few days and keeping my feelings to myself. *But why?* Zina had been a source of comfort during some pretty shitty days since I started working at the bakery.

"I finally told the guy I loved him."

I thought about when William and I said it to each other. *I love you.* It came at such the perfect moment: after he went out of his way for me.

"And how does that feel?" Zina asked.

I stopped in my tracks. "Freeing." I smiled again. I couldn't seem to shake this damn smile.

"See, I knew you'd say it when the time was right. You two seem like such a cute couple. You obviously put a lot of thought and effort into this relationship. Took things slow and look how it's playing out for you."

"He has been there for me so many times. I'm glad I put away my fears wasn't sure if my thoughts were directed toward Zina or in general.

My mind shifted gears and I couldn't help but wonder what the background check would come up with. Would Samuel ever text me back? It had been a few days, and I was hoping Claire had passed on my message. She didn't seem to care for me, but at the same time, I tried to put myself in her shoes. How would I feel if years from now some young girl showed up saying Dayton was her father? Would I be as welcoming?

"Something on your mind?" Zina asked, breaking me out of my stupor.

"Just thinking."

She had her hands on her hips. "I seen that look out of you before, Serenity."

I sighed. "It's just been a busy couple days."

She nodded. "I'm all ears if you need someone to talk to. I don't bite."

I told her about the library, Claire, and what my mom said.

"Wow," Zina whistled, but took it in stride. "That is quite a journey."

I pulled a batch of cinnamon buns out of the oven. "I just don't know what to expect."

"Hmm." Zina appeared lost in thought for a moment. "Do you have a list of questions you'd like to ask him? It's okay to be nervous, but it's also important to prepare, at least emotionally."

My legs trembled. "I have come to accept that if he ever *does* choose to contact me at all, I may not have a relationship with the guy. But I just need closure. I've spent my whole life not knowing who he was."

She placed her hand on my shoulder. "I couldn't imagine, dear."

I forced a laugh. "At least I can say my life isn't boring and that nothing would surprise me." I tried to lighten the mood and cheer myself up. Even after the cluster of bullshit I had experienced recently, I wanted so badly for this to go my way. I wanted Samuel to accept me with open arms. I wanted Mom to be wrong about him. I wanted to believe that he hadn't been there for me for reasons out of his control. It was hard to have one parent who was flaky at best, and then to add a second who, if Mom was telling the truth, couldn't give a damn about me.

During my mid-morning break, I received a text from William: *The background check is done. There is nothing too suspicious. Claire Marrows seems straight, no criminal record, never married, and has lived in the same city for the past twenty years. Samuel lives a few hours from here and has no recent criminal activity within the last ten years.*

I grinned. So Samuel appeared to have gotten his life

together. That gave me a glimpse of hope. Mom was wrong; people changed, and maybe he did for the better.

Thanks, hun, I responded. *I still haven't heard from him. If only I could find another way to contact him.*

I shut off my phone and returned to work. To say I felt relief would have been an understatement, but I still hoped William would have offered some ideas on how to contact Samuel. I had doubts that Claire had passed on my message at all.

As lunchtime approached, the day picked up speed. Work came in waves. It was a nice change of pace since some days dragged on and on, much like life. My life was moving quickly though; there was just so much happening. My mind was filled with so many "what ifs" and thoughts of things out of my control.

"Serenity!" Zina said, coming up to me from the front.

"Yeah?"

"There is a woman here to see you."

I gnawed at my upper lip. "Oh? Did she give a name?" An empty feeling began to develop in my stomach. My muscles twitched.

"She didn't specify, but she said it was important. Don't worry." Zina leaned in and whispered, "You don't need to look concerned. I'll keep an eye out for you."

My nerves lessened a bit. At least she was reassuring.

I walked past Zina to the front. Standing several feet from the till was Claire.

"Hello, Serenity," she said as I approached.

A rolling flutter erupted from my stomach and shot up to my head and down to my toes.

"H— hi," I replied.

"Do you have a minute?"

"Yeah, just give me a second." I turned to go in the back and inform Zina.

I wringed my hands as I passed a co-worker into the back.

I approached Zina. "I need to take a quick break if you don't mind. I really need to talk to her."

She nodded. "Yes, take all the time you need as long as the order gets done."

"Thanks."

I turned and walked back toward the front. Claire had taken a seat by the door.

"We can talk outside." I whispered.

I got a better look at Claire, my supposed aunt, as we walked out the door. Her hair was very curly, similar to mine. It was slightly darker, but there was definitely a familiarity. I paced a few feet from the front door. "Okay, you have my attention."

Claire gnawed at her upper lip. "Samuel said he had been trying to get a hold of you but the number you gave me was out of service. I told you I'd pass your number on, but you made me look like a nut, a fool for even entertaining this suggestion." Claire frowned.

I shook my head. I don't know why or how he got the wrong number. "I gave you my number." I shot off my number slowly again.

Claire backed away, her head shaking vigorously. "Don't blame me. I passed on the number you gave me."

I wiped the sweat from my forehead. "I'm not blaming you, honest." I shuffled from foot to foot. Was she trying to sabotage me? I was positive I gave her the right number. "Besides, if I was playing games, wouldn't I have used a fake name?"

Claire brushed her hair behind her ear casually. "Maybe you're right." She crossed her arms over her chest. "Tell me your number again?"

I rattled off my number a second time.

"Then it doesn't make any sense," she said. "That's the number I passed on."

I was so confused. "Could you try again? It's important."

She sighed and pulled out her cellphone. "He's coming to town this weekend, so maybe I can arrange for a meeting."

I grinned. "Please. I'd love that."

My heart almost pumped out of my chest. William wasn't going to believe my luck.

"I'll text you when I set it up, okay, Serenity?"

I almost reached out to hug her but stopped. "You don't know how much I appreciate this, Claire."

She hmphed. "I have to go."

Without a proper goodbye, she stormed away. I stood there, stunned at what had just happened. What was that? She was an odd duck, that was for sure. Was her brother — my father — anything like her? She was short with me one moment, nice another, then annoyed, and finally abrupt. I couldn't really prepare for how she would act. I never expected her to track me down to my work. Could she have been stalking me? Something just didn't sit well with me; she confirmed the number I gave her, and she was sure she had passed it on correctly. Yet it was wrong. Didn't Samuel double check with his sister when the number didn't work? I hated all of this. I just hoped that Claire would come through.

I returned to work and wasted no time getting my task done. I had spent longer than I should've talking to Claire, and I was behind. Was I in trouble? As I returned to my station, one made eye contact with me Even Zina's normal cheerful demeanor was flattened even though walk-ins were at all-time high today. Maybe it was all in my head, and I needed to just work.

But finally at 1:20 PM — twenty minutes later than I usually left for the day — I could go home. I checked my phone and still had no new message from Claire. I quickly updated William on what had happened earlier. Then I had to make the journey back to my place. I entertained the hope that Sarah, my new roommate, had gone to work or something. If she was there, I'd have to deal with it though. I just hoped that she had sobered up and was a little more tolerable. I started my trudge back to the apartment.

As I walked toward the front door, I stared absently in front of me, focusing on nothing and everything at the same time as I replayed the afternoon events in my mind. I wondered if Claire was secretly as curious about me as I was about my father. She was reluctant but still made an effort to locate where I worked to pass on a message. But a part of me suspected that she wanted to make me feel just as uncomfortable or awkward as she may have felt when I showed up to where she worked. Or the alternative was that I was simply overthinking it all. I hoped it was the latter.

I walked inside my place. This time, Sarah was passed out on the couch. As I headed for my room, Sophia exited the bathroom. "Hey, Serenity." Her hair was an uncombed, chaotic mess.

"I take it you and *her* had quite a fun night last night," I said, jerking my head to where Sarah lay sprawled.

Sophia frowned. "She really isn't that bad. She thinks you don't like her."

I glared at her. The last thing I needed was to live with a

partier. "My first time meeting her, it was evident she had been drinking, so yeah, maybe my first impression of her wasn't great."

Sophia matched my angry gaze. "It's not like that, Serenity."

I stopped myself from rolling my eyes. "Then how is it? Enlighten me. Because honestly, before she moved in here, you were never a partier and I—"

"I broke up with Andre and she thought I needed a distraction," Sophia blurted out. She bit her lip and looked around nervously.

The tension in my shoulders lessened. "Oh, Sophia, I'm sorry." *In time she'll realize it was a blessing in disguise. He was no good, and she did deserve better,* I thought, but bit my tongue instead.

"It was for the best." She clenched her fists. "Men are such pigs."

"Some are, yes." Sophia obviously hadn't spent much time around William. To be fair, it was kind of difficult for her to do so since I never brought him around, but she didn't realize William was one of a kind. He wasn't a pig or a jerk. He was special to me in more ways than one.

She softened her expression. "I'm sorry I yelled at you. How are things going for you? I feel like we haven't talked in forever."

Uh, because you are literally mean to me every time I try to talk to you, I desperately wanted to add. Instead I said, "I'm good."

"Are you planning on staying tonight?"

I nodded. "Yup. William's busy tonight." *Please, stop talking to me!* I wanted to scream.

"Oh, I have an idea!" Sophia clasped her hands together

and then clapped excitedly. "You, Sarah, and I should have a girls' night!"

I cringed at the thought of spending any amount of time with Sophia, let alone spending a night with her and basically a stranger. That was not my idea of fun. Sophia and I had just started to get along after spending the better part of my occupancy here at odds with her and her shitty attitude. So why did she think we were suddenly friends?

"What do you say?" she asked.

"Oh, I don't know. I'm kinda tired..."

"Come on, Serenity, please!" she begged.

I swore to myself on the inside, but I didn't know what to say or how to let her down gently that I wasn't interested. But there she was, standing there and looking so excited that I didn't want to turn her down. Plus, I couldn't think about the last time I went out, and I had some extra money since William had been buying the groceries lately. Still frowning, I just sighed. "Okay, fine, sounds good. But I have to work tomorrow, so we have to be home by midnight!"

"Fine!" Sophie clapped again, grating on my nerves. She started jumping like a giddy little kid. *Great.* "Once Sarah is feeling better we can discuss the details!" She turned and ran back to her room, mumbling to herself, "I wonder if my little black dress is clean... With those heels..."

"Well, right now I'm going to go have a nap," I shouted to her, but she didn't seem to hear me.

I moseyed past her room and into my own, closing the door and locking it. I lay face-first on my bed to check my messages.

A text came across the screen from a number I didn't recognize. *How does this Friday work for you?*

Claire? I texted back.

Who else? came the rude as usual response.

Sorry, yes. Friday is perfect, I quickly replied.

It was official. It was finally official that in less than a week, I'd finally meet my father. I couldn't wait. I did a little dance out of pure excitement, much like I had when William got me a job. When the warm tingly feelings subsided, I texted William the news. I owed all of this to him.

Chapter 14

I woke and sat unsteadily on the edge of the bed. I was meeting Samuel for the first time today. Last night I insisted that William drop me off at home so I could prepare mentally. He would be picking me up to drive me to the meeting place. I wondered if I should tell Mom about meeting Samuel. Since I had talked with her last, contact with her had been intermittent. I knew she was angry. Hurt perhaps, and I wished I could talk to her about it.

A lump formed in my throat. Mom used to tell me I had toads in my throat whenever I got nervous. She liked the play on words even if the analogy wasn't quite right.

I don't appreciate you pulling a fast one. That was the last text I received from Mom just three days ago after I tried to make light of me reaching out to Samuel. I wanted so badly to tell her that if she didn't keep secrets from me, I wouldn't have to lie to get what I needed out of her. For the umpteenth time, I circled my thumb over the screen, trying to formulate a response, but my brain came up short. Anything I'd say to her would likely just piss her off her more. Any reply that wasn't telling her I was giving up on my search or that she was right, she'd take as an insult. She took everything personally.

I swallowed hard and tossed the phone beside me. I needed to get dressed and ready to go. I was nervous and it was clear; William told me last night to just be myself. But what if being myself scared Samuel away? I was a walking disaster. Maybe I'd say the wrong thing and he'd never want to see me again. Maybe he'd live up to Mom's comments, Aunt Jane's comments. Everyone in my family hated the guy. But why?

I quickly changed into some comfy casual clothes and threw my hair back into a ponytail. *Be me. Don't try to be someone you're not. It's unfulfilling, and it's so hard to maintain those appearances.* William's words rang true in my mind. Even Zina had provided me with some reassurance when I texted her last night voicing my concerns.

I retrieved my phone, left my room, locked the door behind me, and headed for the living room. Even though I'd spent a night out with her, I still hadn't gotten a good read on Sarah, the new roomie, which meant I still hadn't developed enough trust to take the lock off my door. While Sophia and Crystal were pains in my butts, they never were untrustworthy.

I walked into the living room. Every light was on, the television was on full blast, and a few empty beer cans and cartons of takeout food were strewn among the coffee table. Sarah liked to party. Sophia even began to drink more now that Sarah was living here. It was a shame. The only time I went to hang out with her and Sarah for that "girls' night," they both tried to shove alcohol down my throat. Maybe it was because Sarah had just turned 21 and Sophia wasn't much older. But I wasn't a drinker. I never really enjoyed getting smashed. William and I enjoyed the occasional glass of wine, but not much beyond that.

I moved some clutter over and propped my feet on the coffee table as I sat down. At least I had some peace. I scrolled through my messages and waited patiently for the text from

William telling me he was here.

Not even a few minutes went by before I heard the bathroom door open and someone stumble out. I groaned. Sophia walked into the living room, hair disheveled and shirt inside-out and on backwards.

"You have fun last night?" I asked.

Sophia shook her head. "Not really." She faked a smile as she slumped into the couch beside me. "How come you're never home anymore?"

She was right. I have been spending more time with William these past few weeks. If no one knew better, they'd think I lived there.

"Well?" she prompted.

I shrugged. "I've just been spending a lot of time with William."

Sophia sighed. "I missed when it was just you, Crystal, and me."

I opened my mouth slightly. I was taken back. I always thought that Sophia saw me as a nuisance and vice versa. "Really?"

She took a deep breath and whispered, "You were right about Sarah."

I held my breath to avoid having to breathe in too much of the strong scent of stale booze. "Oh?" I didn't know how else to respond. Just a few days ago, Sophia was telling me that Sarah wasn't that bad, but now Sophia was all nostalgic and not that crazy about our new roommate.

"My mom is threatening to stop paying my rent," she confided. "She came here yesterday and told me I had let myself go. It all started after *she* came to live here."

I nodded. Crystal didn't exactly tell us who would be our

new roommate. All she said was that she was a girl from school who was looking for a place to live. Which I found really ironic, considering she stayed up all night, and spent all morning in bed.

"Of course, *you* don't notice," she added.

"I notice," I replied. "You can say no to the drinking, you know."

Sophia was barking up the wrong tree if she was looking for sympathy. I had already tried to warn her about drinking, but she didn't want to listen.

"It's so hard when she is the only one to talk to around here," Sophia said.

"Maybe get out of the house and find some hobbies," I added, but it came out harsher than I intended.

Sophia looked away.

Then my phone pinged, rescuing me from the increasingly awkward situation. "I'd love to talk to you further, but I have to go."

"Will you be back tonight?"

I paused for a moment then simply replied, "Maybe." I knew I'd probably spend the night with William again, but a part of me felt a twinge of guilt. It seemed like Sophia needed a friend.

"Well, if you do decide to come home, maybe we can rent a movie."

I was a little surprised at that. "Sounds good. I'll text you later," I said as I opened the front door to leave.

"Okay, bye, Serenity."

I closed the door behind me. *What was that? When did Sophia become so needy?* I shook away the thoughts as quickly as they entered my mind. I couldn't be distracted by other things right now. My main objective was to meet my father.

Once inside the car, William reached over and planted a soft kiss on my forehead. "Good morning, hun."

"Good morning." I smiled.

"Are you ready?"

"Yes."

I stared at my cell phone. Samuel had sent a text to me for the first time last night confirming the location and time. *I'll be at the coffee shop on Miller and Third at 11.* It was a very direct, professional response.

"It'll be fine," he reassured me.

"Thanks," I mumbled.

William pulled away from the curb. The drive was quiet. William had the uncanny ability to know when to give me some much-needed space to think.

The closer we came to the coffee shop where we agreed to meet, the more my mind raced. What would my father be like? What did he look like? I had thought about the possible answers to these questions over and over again. Would he be like Mike? An asshole? A slob? There were so many words to describe that man, and not one was positive. I wanted to believe that Samuel would be decent. Maybe there was an explanation or a misunderstanding to explain why Mom kept him away, or why everyone else in my family also hated him. The little comments about him were ingrained; it might be hard for me to see past them and really *see* who this Samuel was.

William pulled up to the building. "Here we are," he said softly.

I smiled but my hands trembled.

"Do you want me to come in with you?"

I shook my head. "This is something I need to do on my

own."

He nodded. "I'll be out here in case you need to escape. Take as long as you need."

I reached over, pulled him close, and kissed him. We pulled apart, gazing at one another. "I'll see you soon."

I opened the car door and got out. For a moment, I just stood there, taking in deep breaths.

Here goes nothing.

I entered the coffee shop and looked around. There were a few couples spread around. But my eyes stopped at a man sitting alone in the corner. The man was at least in his forties with short, dark brown hair. He shifted uncomfortably when our eyes met. We stared awkwardly at each other for a moment before he stood. I was surprised to find that he was shorter than I thought he'd be. Maybe a good few inches shorter than I had imagined and lanky. He wore a button-up blue, jean jacket and dark navy jeans. I did notice a remarkable resemblance. I had his big brown eyes, same pointy nose, and broad lips.

He had to be my father. There was no way he wasn't.

"Serenity?" he asked softly.

I nodded. "I— It's nice to meet you."

He held out his hand, and we awkwardly shook. "Samuel, but you can call me Sam."

I faked a smile, but I felt a pang of melancholy. I guess I half-expected him to hug me after not seeing me my entire life. But he shook my hand. He treated me like a business prospect. But I couldn't let him see my disappointment.

"Should we sit down?" he asked.

"Yes."

I followed him to the booth where he had been sitting. I glanced out the window at William's car. I flashed him a smile when he looked up from his lap.

I sat down across from Samuel. He sat up straight and his shoulders rose.

"Claire told me you wished to meet me."

"Yes."

"Did Melody put you up to this?" he asked curtly.

My stomach twisted in a million directions. "No!" Suddenly, I was second-guessing myself and why I was here. "She was against it. Why do you ask?"

He grimaced. "No reason."

I tapped my hand on the table. "I wanted to find you all on my own. It just took a bit of searching and lying to my mother to get to that point," I tried to explain, hoping that letting him know it was one hundred percent my idea would loosen him up a bit.

A waitress approached and took our order. The disruption was freeing while I tried to wrap my mind around the first impression of him, of my *father*. So far, he was apathetic if not a little exasperated by my presence. But I couldn't discount him yet. He might just be nervous.

When the waitress brought our beverages, he took a sip. "So what do you do for a living?" he asked.

"I work at a bakery."

He sneered. "So you followed in your mother's footsteps."

"Excuse me? Why do you hate my mother so much?" I asked bluntly. "Better yet, why do you two hate each other in general?"

Samuel clenched his fist and said nothing.

Annoyed, I prodded further. "Here's your chance to tell me your side of the story. Because the things I've heard about you haven't been good."

He softened his posture. "I had no idea you even existed until I heard from Claire. I have to admit, I pretended you gave me the wrong number because I wasn't sure about meeting you. I was afraid of the lies that would be told about me. But since you did reach out, Here's the truth." He took a deep breath. "I know your mother was bitter after our fling ended, but to not tell me she was pregnant..." His voice trailed off, and he mumbled something about being deceived.

Pain blossomed in my chest; the pressure was so intense I struggled to breathe as I shifted in my seat. All this time, Mom told me he was bad news. But she had lied; she had never even given him a chance to be there for me. My hands shook at how angry I was at her.

How dare she? Maybe my life could have been different. Maybe I wouldn't have been tossed from home to home to home.

Samuel looked away as I boiled with rage. "She was jealous," he said finally. He wasn't looking directly at me, and I sensed he wasn't even talking to me directly.

"Jealous?" I gaped at him. No doubt she probably felt rejected, but jealous? Did he replace her with another girlfriend and this was her way to say, "fuck you" to the guy? Surely Mom couldn't have been *that* bitter. There had to be something more.

"Jane is your aunt, correct?" he asked.

I eyed him prudently. "Yeah? She's my mother's sister. Why?"

He looked away. "I shouldn't be telling you this, Serenity. Forget I mentioned her name."

"No, tell me. Please." I hated secrets. I was so sick of everyone hiding something from me.

"Your Aunt Jane told me that Melody— I mean, told me your mother was cheating on me. So I broke up with her. I didn't hear from her for a few years. Then I started a relationship with Jane." He paused. "I'm sorry, Serenity. I shouldn't be telling you this, but I need you to know the truth. I'm not sure what she's told you, but anyway, I started a relationship with Jane. Melody confronted me." The muscles in his face tightened. "Your mother and I got into it. She was screaming in my face. So I pushed her away. She tripped and hit her head. She had me arrested for assault. She even got a restraining order against me. I spent so much on legal bills only to have the charges dropped. Apparently her story on what happened kept changing, and they eventually just dropped the charges because of the lack of evidence. Either way, I haven't seen her since. I broke up with Jane right after. I couldn't deal with those two."

I rubbed the back of my neck. I wasn't sure how I felt about that, especially since he made it sound like they were both angry and both at fault.

"So now you know the truth," he said. "I'm not innocent, and I am not proud of the person I was back then."

It made sense. Jane was bitter over him dumping her, and Mom was angry over the double betrayal from her sister and my father. No wonder she was so bitter and didn't trust anyone. I don't know how I'd react if Harmony tried to break up William and I.

I tried to move past all this information. I wanted to know more about my father. "So tell me about yourself."

He smiled. "Well, I joined the Marines where I then met my late wife, Charlotte. We had a great few years before she got sick." His voice filled with dread and he looked away for a moment. When he looked back, his eyes were glossy. "I was left to raise our two sons."

"Two sons?" I clarified. I had two brothers I'd never met. A whole other family I never got to encounter. "I have brothers? How old are they?" I couldn't contain my excitement. I realized too late that maybe my excitement was inappropriate given that he had just told me that his wife had died.

He grinned at that. "Yes, Chance is nineteen and Robbie is sixteen."

I smiled back. "I'd love to meet them sometime."

"Maybe someday. First I need to tell them about you." His grin faltered and dropped as he said it.

My smile turned upside-down. "Oh?"

Samuel fumbled with the handle of the coffee cup. "I just wanted to meet you first before I told them anything."

I nodded. "It makes sense." It kind of hurt that I was still a secret, but I understood.

"You seem a little sad. Why?" he asked.

"I guess I'm a bit jealous," I admitted. Chance and Robbie got to live with our dad, but I never got the chance. I had only ever lived with Mom and a bunch of random strangers.

"Why?"

"Well, I never got the opportunity to get to know you. I didn't get much of anything." I cracked my knuckles anxiously. Mom prevented me from having a father purely because of her jealousy. She knowingly let me go into foster care when she had the means to give me a father, someone to take care of me, but she didn't.

Tears threatened to emerge.

"What's wrong?" Samuel shuffled in his seat. "Are you okay?"

"Foster care does that to you."

Here I was telling my father — a stranger — all about my life. Was I trying to make him feel guilty? I didn't know what I expected him to do about it. But I wanted someone, anyone to feel how I felt. Mom got her fair share of my guilt. But I couldn't help it; I had to let him know.

He slumped his shoulders. "I'm sorry to hear."

I crossed my arms. "It isn't your fault. You had no idea I even existed."

"Damn Melody," he swore under his breath. "Charlotte and I could have given you a better life. A stable life."

My insides twisted. I was truly in a lose-lose scenario; I could have had a good life with Samuel, Charlotte, and my brothers, but I wouldn't have had a relationship with Dayton and Harmony. Even though we weren't close, they were the closest confidants I had growing up. But Mom took away my right to know my two other brothers. She could have shared me, but she chose not to.

Samuel looked over at me. "I know this is a lot to cover in one day. But maybe we should wrap things up. Process everything, and then if you'd like, we can set up another meeting."

I bit my lip. "Okay." I didn't want to end our meeting, not just yet. It was emotional, how could it not be? He had been honest with me and didn't sugarcoat the truth. Maybe Mom knew about Charlotte and was jealous. Jealous that Samuel had found true love while she was stuck being a single mother. But that didn't explain why Dayton and Harmony also didn't know their fathers.

Samuel rose and once again shook my hand, but this time he gave me a halfhearted hug. At least it was a step up from the simple handshake from before.

"Have a good rest of your day," he said before turning and walking out of the café.

Instead of going outside, I sat back in the booth. So I had finally met him. I finally met my father. I went from having no name to actually meeting the guy in such a short amount of time. He wasn't as bad as I thought. *But where do I go from here?* What could I expect going forward?

I sent a text to my mom: *I just finished having coffee with Samuel.*

I wasn't quite to the point to refer to him as Dad yet.

Soon, William entered the café and sat in front of me. He didn't say anything as he pulled my hands into his.

I smiled and looked at him. "Thanks for helping me find my father." I couldn't ever repay William for everything he had done for me. This man meant everything to me.

"How did it go?" he asked.

"Good," I said sadly.

"It doesn't sound like it."

I exhaled as I told him what Samuel said.

William blanched. "I'm sorry."

"There's nothing to be sorry about. It happened. I'm glad I know the truth. I guess I'm looking forward to meeting my two half-brothers."

"There is always that."

"All I can do is wait until our next meeting," I said. "In the meantime, what would you like to do?"

William stirred a little but said nothing.

"What's wrong?" I asked.

"Wanna go for a drive?" he asked.

"Okay?"

"There is… something I want to ask you."

We walked outside silently and got into the car. As he drove, his lips parted several times as if he was going to say something, but each time fell silent. What was he thinking about?

"What's on your mind?" I finally asked. "Are you feeling okay?"

He lifted one hand off the steering wheel and skimmed his fingertips along his jaw line, clearly deep in thought.

"Don't keep me in suspense." I reached over and touched his thigh.

He jumped slightly. "Serenity, will you move in with me?" he blurted.

I paused and didn't say anything.

"I— I want you to move in with me," he continued. "I mean, we practically spend every day together anyway. Half of your stuff is already at my house, and I just really want to take that step. Only if you want the same thing, that is."

I leaned back, taking it all in. He wanted me to move in with him. The last few months our relationship had really taken off. We went from awkwardly hanging out when we could to me staying over pretty much every night. And now he wanted me to move in! It would save on rent, and I could wake up every morning to my best friend. What more could I ask for?

"Okay," I said finally.

"Is that a yes?" William inquired.

"Yes." That was it, then. I was moving in. For once I didn't have to dwell on the decision. It came naturally for me. And it was exhilarating.

Then I remembered Sophia. Just mere hours before, she was telling me she hated our roommate and wished it could have gone back to just Crystal, her, and me. How would she take the news that I'd be leaving my notice?

William smiled, and it was a smile that spread from cheek to cheek. "That's great." He was so happy.

"It's almost the beginning of the month, so I'll just leave my notice on the first and find a new roommate for Sophia."

William simply nodded. I wasn't sure if he heard me or not; he was in heaven right now.

"William," I said, breaking him out of his stupor.

"Yeah?"

"I should go talk to my roommates. Sophia, as much as she is a pain in the butt, she was having a bad day. I feel bad to spring this on her over text."

William pulled into a nearby parking lot, brought me close, and kissed me. "You are a great woman. Always thinking of others' feelings."

"I try."

"I'll drop you off and pick you up later. I do have some paperwork I can finish up."

"Thanks."

If Sarah wasn't home, then maybe I'd take Sophia up on her offer to hang out. It could be an afternoon-day-in instead of a night-in.

I walked inside and Sophia was slouched on the couch watching television.

"Hey," Sophia said. "Surprised to see you."

I sat beside her, propping my legs on the end table. "I have nothing planned this afternoon. How about you?"

Sophia scratched the back of her neck. "I'm just relaxing, enjoying the peace before Sarah wakes up."

I sighed.

"What's wrong with you? You and William get into a

fight?"

"No," I told her. "But there is something I need to tell you."

Sophia stared at me. "What?"

"I'm giving my notice at the beginning of the month. I'm going to move in with William. He asked me just now, and I said yes."

Sophia glance lowered. "Oh?"

"I know. But I'm giving you a heads up so that you can prepare. Maybe move yourself, find better roommates, or something." I knew it wasn't what Sophia wanted to hear, but it was the truth.

She chuckled. "Can't say I'm surprised what with the amount of time you spend with him."

I grinned sheepishly.

"It's all right, Serenity. You gotta do you."

I felt the pressure leave my chest as I let out a sigh of relief. She took it better than I imagined.

"How about we order a pizza and watch a movie?" she suggested.

"Okay. But we better order and eat before Sarah wakes up."

A devilish smile crossed Sophia's face. "Or we can run away. She'd never know."

I laughed.

Sophia stood from the couch, phone in hand. "What kind of pizza do you want? I got a coupon somewhere."

"Whatever you want."

She left down the hall to order, and I pulled out my cell.

Why are you telling me this? Mom had replied to my earlier message about Samuel.

I just thought you'd want to know. My throat tightened. She was angry, but I was also angry at her.

So did you get whatever you were looking for out of the sperm donor?

My whole body tightened. Fury consumed me.

It was fine, I replied curtly.

I closed out of the phone messages as Sophia walked back into the room. "I ordered a pepperoni and cheese."

I reached in my pocket and pulled out a ten. "Here."

She took it from me. "Thanks."

My phone vibrated again. I half-expected it to be a text from my mom, but it was Samuel. My heart sped up. Was he texting to set up another date?

Hey Serenity. It was nice meeting you today. I'm sorry we had to meet under these circumstances. Ever since I left the café, I've been trying to find a way to tell you this. I know this is the cowardly way to break it to you. I feel sad that I never got to be a part of your life growing up, and I'm sorry that you had such a hard upbringing. But I just don't think we can have any further contact. I can't be the father you want, and I just can't relive that part of my life. I'm so sorry, and I want you to know it isn't you. I hope in time you accept this and know it's for the best. Thanks.

I closed out of my text, as a wave of tears spilled onto my cheeks. No words could describe the knife through the heart, the pain in my chest, and how the air had been suddenly sucked from the room. My mom was right: he was a jerk and a coward. But why? Why couldn't he love me? Accept that I was his daughter?

Sophia stared up at me.

"What's wrong?" she asked.

I wiped away the tears, trying to gain my composure before I told Sophia about my father. I really didn't care who I told.

"I'm sorry."

I shook my head. "Don't be."

I shouldn't be surprised. Mom was right. He had the chance to get to know me, without Mom interfering, without constraint, but he chose to ditch me.

I held my hand, shaking. I was burning.

I guess my mom was right about you. She said you were a coward. I stared at the start of the text message, my arms trembling. She always told me you were no good. That you would never be there for me. Then you get the chance to get to know me, and to let me in to your family. But you chose to be a coward. You couldn't deal with your own guilt so you run way. But running way doesn't make me disappear. Doesn't make you less of shitty father. You had your chance, but I'll never give you another. You won't hear from me again.

I sent the text, and dropped the phone beside me. I took several heavy deep breaths. I didn't need him in my life. I needed to keep telling myself that.

Chapter 15

I thought his rejection would have hurt less, but I eventually was able to move on. A month later, my life was good — peaceful and going in the right direction. But it was heartbreaking to know that Samuel Robertson, the man I couldn't even stand to refer to as my father, perfectly embodied the description Mom had given him: "Nothing but a sperm donor." She hadn't asked how my meeting went and I didn't tell her. She hadn't really texted me much since I told her that I was going to meet him. I assumed that she felt resentment, sadness, and maybe a little bit of jealousy. I kept replaying my one and only meeting with him in my mind. It went better than I assumed it would. He answered most of my questions and was even ready to introduce me to my half-brothers. Then *poof*, he cut contact with me.

I lounged on the couch in William's apartment, *our* apartment. I still hadn't gotten used to this space now being mine as well. I had a week left at my old place, but most of my stuff was already inside this tiny space. William didn't seem to mind that all my things were everywhere. I also didn't realize just how much *stuff* I had. I turned on the television to drown out the thoughts swarming inside my head.

I leaned back and kicked my legs up to rest on the coffee table, letting my mind drift. The cooking channel was on in the background. Some lady was talking about how to make the perfect donut. Ironically, that was the thing that brought William and I together. I pulled out my phone and texted William.

Can you bring home some donuts? Glazed. Just like old times.

A few minutes later, the much-anticipated reply flashed across my screen. *What's the occasion?*

I smiled. *You and I. We're the occasion.*

I closed out of the message and clicked into the internet browser. I typed in "Samuel Robertson," but this time I included his late wife's name as well. I wasn't sure why I was punishing myself. He made it clear that he didn't want me to be part of his life. He was sorry, he had said. But how sorry could he be?

The first thing to pop up was an obituary. He was telling the truth about his wife. I stared at the woman, my stepmother, or at least she would have been if I had been given the chance to get to know her. The woman in the colorful picture had a broad smile and big, blue eyes. It was like she was looking right at me. She had curly, red hair, much like my mom. In fact, Charlotte shared many similarities with Mom. Samuel had a type, which was red-haired women. But what was it about Charlotte that made her so special and not my mom?

I closed out of the browser without looking for more information. I was doing it again, fantasizing about what could have been. I couldn't help it. Even at 24-years-old, it was normal for a girl to want her parents to be together. Samuel had gone from Mom, to Aunt Jane, to this Charlotte woman.

A bitterness formed in my mouth. I was being rather

unfair to the deceased woman, someone who didn't know me. Yet, deep down, I was blaming her for something that wasn't even in her control. I hated Samuel Robertson for filling my heart with all this deep anger. He had a choice to be a part of my life and he decided not to.

My phone vibrated again. It was William.

There is this new cream-cheese-filled donut a co-worker was telling me about. Would you like to try it?

I giggled. *Of course.*

William and his donuts.

I scrolled through my messages until I stopped at the last one Samuel sent me. William told me to delete it. He said it'd be easier to let go if I didn't have that reminder kicking me in the face every time I used my phone. But I couldn't. Or I didn't want to. This was the last contact I'd ever have with my father. Even through all the mixed emotions, I still wanted to hold on.

Then I stopped at my last message to Mom. She asked me how work was doing. It was so casual. I didn't want casual.

How are you doing today Mom? I sent her.

Mom had been right about Samuel, but my pride was pulling me in two, threatening to rip me apart from the inside. I didn't want to hear, "*I told you so.*" But I still wanted to let her know that she was right and that I was sorry for not listening to her. I was torn.

I'm baking cookies… I was going to call you, but I forgot, she replied.

It's okay. I have been meaning to as well. Only I didn't forget. I was just avoiding her. I wasn't keeping my promise of making more of an effort.

So what's on your mind? Mom replied.

I took a deep breath and whispered, "Here goes nothing."

You were right about him. And I'm sorry for what he did to you. I'm sorry for even trying to locate him in the first place.

I pressed send as quickly as possible. I needed to do it before I changed my mind like the other hundred times I had attempted to tell her.

What exactly did he say he did? Because he did a lot of shit.

He said he assaulted you and started dating Aunt Jane. I didn't want to tell her what else he told me about her.

At least he is honest… But from the sound of things he wasn't all he was cracked up to be.

No! I replied. *But it's okay. I met him. Now I can move on.*

We sent a few more texts back and forth before William walked through the door. Relief washed over me instantly and I put down the phone.

I wrapped my arms tightly around William's body and whispered sweet nothings into this ear. He awkwardly leaned over to put down the box of donuts and proceeded to embrace me.

"Someone's in a good mood," he said.

I smiled and stared deeply into his eyes. My heart was dancing. "I'm just really glad to see you."

"I'm really glad to be coming home to you." His eyes gleamed and the corner of his mouth turned upward.

"What about those donuts?" I asked. What better way to enjoy his presence than to share a sugary treat with him?

He grinned cheek-to-cheek as he reached for the box and handed me a donut. "Just like old times." He handed me one of those cream-cheese-filled ones. I took a bite and I was in heaven. Much like how I was for my entire relationship with William.

"You like?" he asked.

I nodded as he took a bite of his own.

"Do *you* like?" I returned the question.

He stopped to think for a moment. "Yeah." Another pause. "But not as good as the ones that you make."

I smiled. He was in a relationship with a baker, so I'd hope I made the best baked goods. Just like I'd expect him to do my taxes. Fair trade. Even though I was in his debt forever.

He picked up another donut and shoved it in his mouth. "Good idea on ordering donuts. Man, I could eat them all."

I scowled. He stopped mid-bite. I laughed, but he laughed nervously.

"I really do like the cream-cheese-filling. So I think I might have to replicate the recipe," I said.

William's eyes opened wide.

I stood. "I'll be right back." I blew him a kiss as I headed for the bathroom.

I sat on the toilet seat lid and took a deep breath. As much as I loved William's presence, I still had unfinished business with Mom. I still had more I wanted to say to her. My biological father, as much I wanted to just accept it and move on, was on my mind. He wanted nothing to do with me, so all I had left was Mom.

William and I are probably staying in tonight, I had replied to Mom's last text about what I was doing.

Oh? How are you and him doing? she replied.

Remember I told you I was moving in with him. Most of my stuff is already all over his place.

It was weird; I still hadn't met anyone from William's family, and besides my brother — and I guess the aunt I never knew I had — he hadn't meant any of mine. At least the members that meant anything to me.

I hope one day to meet William, my mom texted.

When I get some vacation time, we'll make a trip down.

I sighed. Mom never did move to the city I lived in. She told me that she and Mike found a place a few hours from where they were living before. At least it was closer than before but still far away enough that I couldn't just hop in the car and drive there on a whim.

And make sure to bring him with you. Promise, Mom texted.

I will Mom, I promise, I replied.

Mom was all I had left. If anything she surprised me. Not once did she rub it all in my face. She was right about Samuel; he was a jerk. Maybe life would have been different if Mom had told him about me, but it didn't change the fact that *now* he had a chance to know me and he chose to reject me. That was no longer on Mom; that was all on him.

I love you Mom. I texted.

I love you too sweetie. I hope to see you soon. And maybe even get you three kids together. I know I say that a lot. But I hope it happens soon.

Me too.

I want you to know I love you Serenity. I'm sorry I wasn't there for you growing up. But I'll try. She replied.

I sat there. Mom wasn't perfect. I realized I had such high expectations for her, I'd get mad and nothing she did was enough. But after what my father did to me. What a coward he was, my expectations were lowered. At least Mom tried, as little or as disappointing her efforts were.

You are the only Mom I have. Please stop beating yourself up over the past. Neither of us can change it. I'm looking forward to the future, and I'd love for us to both move on and enjoy each other's company in the present. I replied.

She was my mother. The only parent I had. It was either I take what I had, or let her go. I remembered Zina's wisdom. She was right. I'd let go of the outcome, and have a relationship with Mom. If that meant seeing her once a year, or talking a few days a week, then I guess that was what I'd have to settle with.

Okay, sweetie I'll try.

I smiled and sent a final reply. You have a great rest of your day, I'll talk to you later.

I put away my phone and exited the bathroom.

I put my phone away and exited the bathroom.

William paced back and forth, his hands in his pockets. He stopped abruptly when he saw me. He fiddled with the collar of his shirt.

"What's wrong?"

"Nothing."

I approached him and touched his shoulder lightly. He jumped.

"Did I do something wrong?" I asked.

He gulped, and without a word he fumbled in his pockets and pulled out a small box with a little ribbon attached.

"I— I got you something," he said nervously.

"Oh?"

My heart began to speed up. *Could it be? Could he really be doing what I think he's doing?* I loved him, but I wasn't ready for that.

My mind fumbled at all the possibilities. Moving in was a big step, but I didn't want to risk moving too fast. If anyone would understand that, it would be William. Right?

He opened the box and pulled out a ring. It had a heart-shaped topaz in the center. It was my birthstone. The band was a classic gold, simple and elegant. It was beautiful. It was thoughtful. It was perfect.

He took my hand and slipped the ring on my finger. "I love you." He pronounced each word slowly and softly. "These past few months, we have grown as a couple. I've grown a fondness for you that I hadn't had for any other woman. After you accepted moving in with me, it solidified that next step in our relationship — a big step for both of us. So I wanted to solidify our relationship. I wanted to give you this promise ring as a promise to be there for you." Tears brimmed his eyes.

I brought my hand to my chest, my mouth open, and my own tears welling up and threatening to fall. "I— I don't know what to say."

"Do you like it?"

I wrapped my arms around him. "Like it? Don't you mean love it?"

He released a satisfied sigh, brushed his hand along my cheek, leaned in, and kissed me. "I was worried you wouldn't like it."

I placed my hands on his shoulders and gazed into his eyes. "I'd love anything you gave me. You don't know how thoughtful you are, and how much I appreciate you for everything you do."

"Just wait there," he said and then disappeared into the kitchen. He was back a moment later with a bottle of champagne. It was covered in beads of icy water. "I think we should make a toast to celebrate a new beginning in our lives together," he said looking at me lovingly with that now-familiar little grin.

We sat back down on the couch with our arms around each other for a few minutes, gazing into each other's eyes. Then William popped the cork out of the bottle and poured its bubbling contents into the two glasses that sat on the table in front of us.

We clinked the glasses together and laughed as the

champagne bubbled and spilled over down the sides. It was a magical moment. The initial suspense, William's earnest expression, the ring, the champagne, and the vows we made of our enduring relationship, it was all perfect. What lies ahead? I didn't know for sure, but I suspected that it was going to be better than I had ever expected.

www.ingramcontent.com/pod-product-compliance
Lightning Source LLC
Chambersburg PA
CBHW030248130626
46549CB00002B/436